THE SCHOLAR, THE SPHINX AND THE SHADES OF NYX

Book One
The Scholar and the Sphinx Series

By
Alison Reeger Cook

KNOX ROBINSON
PUBLISHING
London • New York

KNOX ROBINSON
PUBLISHING
3rd Floor, 36 Langham Street
Westminster, London W1W 7AP
&
244 5th Avenue, Suite 1861
New York, New York 10001

Knox Robinson Publishing is a specialist, international publisher of historical fiction, historical romance and medieval fantasy.

Printed in the United States of America
and the United Kingdom.

First published by KRP in Great Britain in 2013.
First published by KRP in the United States in 2013.

Cover design by Grzegorz Rekas

Typeset in Minion by Susan Veach
info@susanveach.com

Download the KRP App in iTunes and Google Play to receive free historical fiction, historical romance and fantasy eBooks delivered directly to your mobile or tablet.

Watch our historical documentaries and book trailers on our channel on YouTube and download our podcasts in iTunes.

www.knoxrobinsonpublishing.com

David gasped as he felt the painfully cold water envelope his legs, icing over. It continued up his body, cocooning him, drenching him in the stark numbness of night. It permeated through his clothes, through his skin, into the trails of his veins, soaking up the warmth of his blood and chilling it, causing everything inside to ache and scream. He struggled to keep his head up, but the water was crawling up around his chest, around his neck ... he could just make out muffled words of anguish calling for him through the water clogging his ears ... and then it washed over his face ...

CHAPTER ONE

It takes only one reckless decision to change a life—to better it, worsen it, or end it. It takes only one decision to make someone a hero, or a fool. It was that kind of decision that led a young man to journey into the Curtain, outwit a predator, befriend a shape shifter, face the test of an ancient spirit, confront a goddess, and be loved by one of the most infamous monsters in the world. This is how it happened.

Surrounded by his citadel stacks of books, David Sandoval devoured words on a printed page as one consumes the most treasured of treats. Much like the biblical king for which he was named, he ruled over his designed realm of knowledge, a kingdom constructed from everything he found engrossing, from swordplay, to history, to languages, and most devotedly, to the tales of the supernatural and magical. No one could understand why such fairy tales fascinated David so—his family considered it "impractical," and concluded it was only a phase—but his stories of mythical beasts and enchanting spirits had given him quite a reputation in the city of Cervera. He always tried to sneak something unusual into any conversation, or give advice to others based on what a legendary hero would do. He wrote all of his ideas and stories down in journals, away from disapproving glances or patronizing gossip. Unfortunately, David experienced none of the excitement that he wove into his stories, for nothing frightening or wonderful happened in his hometown.

He came from a long line of tradesmen, less whimsical, more practical people. His father was a hard worker who was adequate enough at his job for his family to live comfortably. It had been hard times in Cervera, since its famous university had been relocated to Barcelona when David was only six years old, and this had triggered a great economic strain on the city. The Sandoval family was not in dire straits, however, and could not rightfully complain—even if it made David's parents crestfallen that their children would not as easily get the advanced education they had hoped for before losing the university. David's father, being a pious man, was the one responsible for naming David after the Biblical king that had overcome the giant Goliath, setting the expectation that his son should always conquer any insurmountable obstacle that life would present. David held his pride in being named after a king, as he knew from the old tales that one's status in life, and his prosperous future, was tied to having a meaningful name.

The opportunity for a prosperous future arrived in the form of a letter shortly after David's sixteenth birthday, one of the many milestones he anticipated for the year 1852. He tore ecstatically into the letter, knowing it was a reply to his request for apprenticeship in Paris. He was to study under the renowned architect Antoine Roland, a long-time friend of the Sandoval family.

This is an exciting time for Paris, as it is undergoing a grand modernization, Monsieur Roland wrote in his eloquent and loquacious letter to the Sandovals. *Napoleon Bonaparte III has great plans to rejuvenate the city, and under the direction of Baron Haussmann, I am one of an exclusive selection of engineers commissioned to help with new layouts for Paris's streets and public parks. Such a large scale endeavor is a great opportunity for any aspiring architect, and I know that David would be the perfect apprentice to assist me in this project.*

David was inflated with a burst of delight at these words. This was his ticket to an admirable career and wealth of which his father and brothers could only dream.

His delight was abruptly deflated once his mother told him that they had sent for the eldest son of their neighbors, the Guerreros, to be David's traveling companion.

"No! Not Pablo!" David begged. "Mother, he hates me!"

"Of course he doesn't hate you. Pablo has nothing but respect for you," his mother insisted. "It is dangerous for a boy as young as you to travel on his own. There are thieves on the roads, and swindlers in the towns. Pablo is older and stronger."

Pablo was a bulky braggart of a fellow, strong in arms but not so much in brain, which was a severe contrast to David's lean, limber stature and erudite mind. While Pablo wasn't smart, he could be charismatic when he desired to be, and he often deceived Señora Sandoval into thinking he was an upstanding man. David knew better, as all the childhood years of Pablo flicking him behind the ears, giving him hard punches in the shoulder, and tripping him into mud puddles were not forgotten nor forgiven.

"Mother, have I not proven that I am mature and smart beyond my years?" David said. "I know how to protect myself. I will always keep my belongings in my sight. I will send letters home every day if you want me to, and I will not take any detours. Please, mother, I'm not a child! Give me a chance. If I am to prove myself to Monsieur Roland, I need to show him I can take care of myself and be responsible. How can I do that if I need to be chaperoned to Paris?"

It took several days of insistence and the consent of his father—"I was traveling on my own when I was his age," Senor Sandoval noted—and David's mother finally relented. She made him promise to send letters home at every stop along the way, and she made no promises not to send Pablo after him if her mother's intuition should alert her to trouble.

David was so thrilled that even his mother's threat could not ruin his mood. He would be traveling to Paris, without parents or chaperones to tell him what to do. This was going to be the best time of his life.

David arrived in the city of Orléans, about 81 miles southwest of Paris, by carriage after a long, tiring week of travel. The carriage driver dropped him off at an inexpensive inn to spend the night, the Villa Valere, and David unloaded his baggage with words of thanks to the driver. He entered the inn, where he was greeted by the innkeeper and his multitude of freely roaming dogs. A playful hound bounded up to David, almost knocking him over. David placed his baggage down to pat the dog on the head. While a young bellboy took his packs to his room, David settled down at a small table in the dining area, and ordered an inexpensive supper of bread and cheese, topping it off with a glass of wine. He did not normally drink wine, but how could he resist, now that Mother and Father were not there to dictate his decisions?

The whispers of music wafted into the inn from outside. It sounded strange to David, and he couldn't place the melody or the style. "Innkeeper, where is that music coming from?" he asked in French. He had done his best to brush up on his French before his trip, but his Spanish accent made it obvious that it was not his first language.

The innkeeper glanced up at him, and turned his head towards the inn's entrance. "A caravan of performers set up their act at the end of the street. They pass through every now and then. Quite amusing. You should take a look."

"Just keep your coin purse close. Got to be watchful of sticky fingers," murmured a patron at a table in the corner of the room. He was a wiry old man, grizzled and gaunt, his head hovering just inches above the tabletop while his hand clutched desperately onto his wine bottle. Another man sat with him, buried inside a coat that was too large for him and a hat that swallowed his scalp, and observed the room in silence.

"Come now, Gustav. They're harmless folk," the innkeeper replied.

"Ha! Harmless, he says," Gustav choked up a laugh, and took a drink. "Gypsies are never harmless. Rob you blind, at the least. Give you the evil eye, curse you with their black magic."

The coat-cocooned man gave Gustav a light shove. "Hush, old man." He turned to David. "Don't mind him. He's scatterbrained even when he's not drunk."

David shrugged. "I'm not afraid of gypsies. They're only people, like us."

Gustav lifted his head, and a crooked grin sliced across his face. "Oh, you think so? I hear they like to steal children, straight out of their beds in the night. Turn them into animals, or sell them to the witches and nasty spirits." He raised his hands, waving his fingers at David in a spell-casting motion, and puckered his lips to let out a slurred, "Ooooooooh."

Gustav's friend gave him a hard smack in the shoulder. "No more stupid ghost stories."

David shook his head. "Even if that were true, I have nothing to worry about. I'm not a child, after all."

Gustav looked David up and down. "Not so much a man yet, either," he snickered.

David glowered, and turned away from the two men. He did his best to not appear bothered by the old man's opinion of him. Eventually, his undeniable curiosity nipped his ankles to rouse him to his feet, coaxing him out of the inn and down the street. A wondrous display was set up: three massive painted wagons of brilliant colors and designs formed a triangle, with draperies and banners and paper decorations entwined together. Round flower-patterned lanterns illuminated the square, and music poured from the instruments of the minstrels wearing fine costumes. Gypsy dancers twirling scarves entertained passersby, and the women and children went about selling jewelry, bottles, ornaments, and charms from baskets. Two of the carts had been opened into stage platforms; upon one, a well-toned man juggled flaming torches, and on the other a young boy performed simple magic tricks. The caravan had drawn quite a crowd, and the townspeople threw coins and applauded the performing artists. Children came around to pet the six burly white horses that drew the caravan.

Even before having heard the drunken man's warning at the inn, David was not entirely trusting when it came to gypsies. They were considered swindlers, con artists, and tricksters, and some people thought even worse of them. Many towns had already banned nomadism, but since the emancipation of the gypsies from slave bondage, many bands of them were migrating across Europe. Being the reader of paranormal tales as he was, David knew plenty of stories about gypsies who were, underneath their pretty visages, witches or even were-animals. There was only one book that he had read that painted them in a kinder light, one by a French writer named Victor Hugo—it was a story about a hunchback who fell in love with a kindhearted gypsy girl—but it wasn't as captivating as the shape-shifter folklore that David loved. Yet, he had to admit, the gypsies were fine artists. Their music was mesmerizing, and the dancers were—aside from inappropriately flirtatious—nice.

A dark-eyed gypsy spotted David, and she walked over to him with a coy smile. Her outfit was adorned with colorful beads and jangling gold coins, and her long black hair blossomed with ribbons and silk flowers. She carried a basket full of random knick knacks. *"Bonjour,"* she cooed in hesitant French. *"Voulez-vous acheter?"*

David could tell by the way she had asked, "Would you like to buy?" that she had been trained what to say, and most likely she didn't understand French. *"Hablas español, señorita?"* he offered, wondering if Spanish would be an easier language for her.

Judging by the confused look on her face, apparently it was not.

"English, perhaps?" David asked her.

A smile bloomed on her face, and she nodded. "Yes, English is better. Perhaps you would like to buy something? I have many exotic charms from faraway lands. They are unlike anything else in the world."

David instinctively placed his hands over his trousers' pockets, before she had a chance to pluck something from him without his knowing. While logic dictated that he should walk away, his incorrigible curiosity kept him locked in place. "Sorry, but I don't need anything. You had better move on."

"I may have something that would be perfect for you." The girl dug deep into her basket, producing a stylish old-fashioned dagger in a black and silver sheath. It curved like a basilisk's tongue. "This was custom made by a highly praised blacksmith in Arabia. Here, you may look at it if you like."

David took the dagger, removing the blade a few inches from its sheath before sliding it back in. "This is a fine piece of work," he admitted. "But I'm sure that it is out of my price range."

"But look at the way it sits in your hand. It is a perfect match. I will sell it at a special price, just for you. Fifteen francs. Such a rare piece would cost thrice that much."

David paused, calculating if he had the money to spare. For the girl to sell the dagger that cheaply, it must be of low quality, but it was always useful to have a blade. With a sigh, he held the dagger out to the girl. "I'm sorry, I really shouldn't."

"Then how about a game instead?" A voice, thick with a Scottish brogue, ambushed David from behind. David snapped his head around to see a burly man, with copper red hair thick on his head and face, and a brazen smile that would make wolves cower at the sight of his teeth. The man wore a dark green vest with no shirt, and the muscular masses of his arms and shoulders made David's slim physique comparable to a blade of grass. David realized that this was the juggler who had been performing onstage earlier.

"A game?" David squeaked.

"You seem to be a bright fellow. You win, the dagger's yours."

David gulped. "And if I lose?"

The Scotsman chuckled. "Then you walk away as you are now, no better or worse. Nothing to lose. How's about it, lad? Even a wee bairn could win this game."

By now, the conversation had attracted the attention of the crowd around them. People pressed in, murmuring in excitement. David cast his glance around, looking for a way to escape. When he didn't respond to the juggler's invitation, the crowd spoke up, urging David to accept the challenge. They began to chant and clap, and the gypsy performers encouraged it. David blushed so red, he was sure his clothes would burst into flame from the heat in his face. Finally he nodded in assent. The people cheered as the juggler clasped one of his great arms around David's shoulders and dragged him up onto one of the stages.

The Scotsman went over to a barrel on the side of the stage and took out three large juggling clubs.

"I don't know how to juggle," David said meekly.

The juggler laughed. "You don't have to juggle. You only have to sit."

David felt a weight lifted from his body. "Is that all? Sitting?"

"For as long as you can. I'm wagering … twenty seconds. You manage longer than that, you win."

"Why would I only be able to sit for twenty—"

The juggler came over to David, turned around so that his back was towards him, and knelt down. "Hop up," the Scotsman said.

"Hop up? On your back?"

"On my shoulders, boyo. I said you'd be sitting, not clinging to my backside like a monkey."

David took a deep breath, which he instantly regretted because the musk of the Scotsman was enough to make a skunk pass out. He awkwardly lifted one leg up and placed it over the juggler's right shoulder, and it took him three or four hops before he could successfully swing his other leg up. He was barely in place before the juggler stood up abruptly, and David struggled not to fall off. The people in the audience laughed at David's shaky shifting, but once he found his balance, he relaxed his muscles. This wasn't so bad. How was this game a challenge?

Another gypsy walked up on the stage, holding an oil lamp. The juggler touched each club to the lamp's flame, and they ignited in wickedly dancing flames. David's eyes opened to the size of tea saucers at the sight of the burning clubs.

"Sit as straight as you can," the juggler advised. "Don't lean back, and don't lean forward. And don't sneeze. Last fellow who did this sneezed in the middle of the act. I hope the poor bloke's hair grew back."

For the first time that day, David's curiosity was nowhere to be found. In its place was a voice in his head screaming, *Get out of there, you idiot!*

But he couldn't. The juggler launched into his act before David could demand to be put down, as the burning torches flew up only inches from David's face. The flames rose and danced around David, trails of orange tongues licking at the air around his head. The boy's skin, usually the color of cream-cooled coffee, blanched to milk white, while his brain willed for Time to pick up its pace.

Then there was a fourth club—more specifically, a butcher knife. Then a cleaver. Then a machete. The assisting gypsy stood off to the side, tossing blades to the juggler, who caught them in mid-pass and added them to his twirling tornado of torture. The audience held its breath as the juggler increased speed, catching and releasing his implements while David sat petrified, his hair standing on end. As David was about to scream for deliverance from this death trap, the blur of fire and flashing metal stopped.

"Thirty seconds! Well done, lad!"

The next thing he knew, David was back down on the stage, planted securely on his feet. He felt something pressed into his hand, and it took him several moments to regain his wits to realize it was the dagger—his prize. He looked up to see the gypsy girl, who gave him a quick congratulatory kiss on the cheek. The crowd was cheering and applauding, but David couldn't hear it. His head was still spinning as the juggler guided him off the stage, patting him roughly on the back.

"Not bad, boyo. I was sure you would be screaming for your mum before time was up. You have thicker skin than I thought." The juggler shook David's hand, giving him a smile that seemed less genuine than before, even tinged with a bit of irritation.

That was when David noticed the tattoo on the juggler's arm: a silver spear standing straight in the middle, with two golden arrows crossing behind it, and a white lily wrapped around the head of the spear. The Master Huntsmen's crest.

The exclusive guild of the most exceptional hunters in the world had intrigued David ever since he had heard about them from his uncle, who, admittedly, claimed to always know more than he truly did. David himself would have liked to give hunting a try, but his mother had adamantly protested, calling it a barbaric sport not suitable for a refined young gentleman.

Was it possible that the juggler had once been a Master Huntsman? No, he couldn't be. The tattoo must be a facsimile. After all, who would give up the excitement of being a Huntsman to be a second rate juggler?

David's room at the inn was small, only a stiff bed, a bedside table and one window, but it was enough. Sleep eluded David that night, the adrenaline from his near-death encounter keeping him awake, so he lay in bed reading his books. He had become enthralled in one story by a writer named Johann Ludwig Tieck, about a woman named Brunhilda who was brought back to life by a sorcerer and then went about drinking the blood of children. Heaven only knew why David wanted to indulge in a horror story after the evening he had been through, but he could not put it down. The story tainted his paranoia enough, however, that he removed his new dagger from his pack and stuck it under his mattress. His logical mind knew that no demon named Brunhilda was going to pay him a visit, but he recalled hearing a superstition about how placing knives under one's mattress or pillow was an effective ward against evil and bad dreams.

It was after midnight when David finally felt sleep seeping into his bones. He settled into bed and extinguished his bedside candle. He was just about to fall asleep when a sudden draft blew open his window's shutters, causing them to flap and clap like wooden wings in the breeze. That was odd, he must have not locked his windows well enough, although he was certain he had latched them shut. He got up and closed the shutters again, confirming the lock was secure.

Once he returned to bed, his eyelids began to droop again, but then he caught the scent of something. It was pleasant, soothing, like the odor of herbal tea. He could tell this new smell was too strong to be wafting up from the inn's kitchen. It was like the source of the smell was right there, in that room with him. Yet panic did not seize him; the delightful smell calmed him, drawing him into a state of contented relaxation.

Blurry visions of wonderful colors and shapes passed through his mind, and a soft tinkling of bells filled the air. He smiled a little, a tiny hum of peace escaping his throat. He enjoyed it for about another minute until his consciousness slapped him to attention. The tinkling sound was very close to him, as if someone were jingling coins next to his ear, and something was pressing down onto his body. A touch alighted on his cheek. He shot his eyes open, and although he could not see his intruder, he could feel a hot breath warming his face.

Something was right on top of him.

Horror grasped David's entire body. The word "vampire" rang loudly in his ears. He had no wooden stake or cross on him—not that it would have done any good, given that he couldn't move. David cringed on the inside and the intruder sniffed gently on his nightshirt collar. He could hear his blood pounding in his ears, and he knew any moment his assailant was going to bury its teeth into his neck.

His mind grasped for logic long enough to remind him: *the dagger ... under your mattress ...*

David swung his leg around and kicked the thing in the side. It huffed and reeled back, startled. He kicked it again, this time digging his heel into its neck, sending the intruder tumbling off the bed onto the floor. He flipped out of bed and thrust his hand under the mattress, quickly pulling out his dagger. He ripped it from its sheath and held it up threateningly. But rather than attack him, the creature burst out the window, nearly breaking the shutters right off their hinges.

David rushed to the window, looking out into the empty expanse of sky. He lowered his dagger, wondering how the animal could have disappeared so fast. His foot bumped into something, and when he looked down, he saw his coin purse on the floor.

He was baffled. He was sure his purse had been in his trouser pocket, which was tucked away in his traveling case. Had his assailant been trying to rob him?

As he traced his fingers along the windowpane, noting the scratches that had been left behind in the wood, he found something small caught in one of the gouges. It was a thumbnail-sized gold coin, a decorative piece, much like the ones worn by the gypsy girl who had given him the dagger. His attacker must have been wearing a good number of these coins from the jingling sound he had heard. David knew where to go to find that creature, and learn what manner of demon it may be.

The next day, David wasted no time searching out the gypsy caravan. The gypsies had already packed up and left town before dawn, but he couldn't imagine they had gone too far. He asked around the market if anyone had seen where the caravan had departed to, but no one knew. Eventually he stumbled upon the grocer's shop. The caravan folk had purchased a good amount of eggs, bread, flour and milk before heading off towards a grove on the other side of the river. The grocer mentioned that whenever the caravan passed through the area, they tended to stay a few days in that particular grove before moving on. So it was the place to start. Before he left the grocer, he bought a string of garlic cloves, just for good measure.

It was late evening when David left the inn and made his way through the dusk-washed streets of Orléans. He did not want the gypsies to hear him approaching by horse or in a carriage, so he decided he would walk to the grove and sneak up on foot under the cloak of night. That way, he could peek in and gauge the situation in the caravan's camp. He did not fear roadside thieves that could be lurking nearby; he had his dagger with him, although he predicted his most effective weapons that night were going to be the garlic-clove necklace around his neck and the makeshift wooden cross in his pocket. He also had a few other small items that he had collected throughout the day, secured in a leather pouch on his belt. He thought they would be helpful against demons and undead adversaries: a hand mirror, a silver spoon, some corks, a needle, and a shaker of salt. The walk was a good distance, but eventually David arrived at the river and crossed the bridge, and night's shadow settled with sudden swiftness around him.

He soon caught a glimpse of ghostly light emitting from an opening in the trees not far away. Standing up and advancing cautiously, David approached the clearing. The light flickered from a bonfire, flashes of orange, scarlet and yellow dancing on the trees. There was a collection of caravan wagons, placed here and there around the grove like a small town, their painted sides taking on demonic images in the coating of red from the fire.

All around the grove were the snoozing gypsies. Scattered among them were sleeping dogs, cats, some goats and a handful of small sheep. The forest floor they lay upon was covered in soft cushions and rugs, giving the appearance of a room in a palace. One wagon in the middle of a large nestled group had one of its sides pulled down into a theatrical stage, standing about a foot above the ground. The walls of the wagon's interior room were adorned in dozens of long colorful drapes, and in the center was a smooth bronze bowl, ten feet in diameter and about four feet deep.

David tiptoed around the sleeping people. He looked up towards the massive bronze bowl, with the edges of satin pillows spilling over it. David pulled his dagger from his belt and cautiously ascended into the wagon.

Thoughts of concern entered his mind. Why was he doing this? He wasn't really sure what he was up against, and he might do himself more harm than good. Besides, if these gypsies were already set on leaving the area, why not just let them go, along with whatever strange creature they were hiding? David told himself, *because that creature could have killed me—possibly.* Wherever this caravan goes, the beast might continue searching for victims, and may be more successful in killing one next time. He felt in his gut that this needed to be done.

Plus, it all was rather exciting. David the Monster Slayer—it had a nice ring to it.

He raised his dagger over his head as he peered over the edge of the bowl. He halted, every muscle in his body tensing into stillness, except for his eyes that widened and his jaw that went slack. It was no vampire or hell beast, but the soft shape of a youthful woman. Except for her head and shoulders, she was mostly buried beneath her nest of pillows and fur blankets. Her dark cascading hair and her throat were adorned with gypsy-woven strands of gold, silver, and jewels, and a light scarf of white wrapped around her chest, looping up around her neck. Her skin was golden tan, close to the color of sun-drenched sand, and it was smooth like glass. What caught David the most was her face; it was unlike any he'd ever seen. It was a face that was feral, yet at the same time so delicate, that David was filled with both trepidation and fascination.

He stared bewildered at the sleeping woman, and then cast his gaze around the caravan. He wondered, for a moment, if he had been completely mistaken about his theory. Granted, this woman could be of the netherworld, and he had not ruled out the possibility of vampirism. Vampires, according to his readings, were noticeably of the undead—pale, ghostly, and reeked to high heaven of decay. They were also supposed to sleep in coffins, not out in the open like this. Still, she could be some kind of demon. He removed the cross from his pocket and held it up to the woman, preparing for any volatile reaction she might make to its presence. She did not awaken. He leaned over the bowl's rim and held the cross a little closer, almost an inch from her serene face, but nothing happened. He pulled away and shoved the cross into his trouser pocket, admitting to himself that he was a little disappointed. Maybe the creature he was looking for was not even here. David began to think perhaps more research was in order, and was ready to turn around and sneak away, when he glanced back at the sleeping woman and saw that she was wide awake, staring at him.

With very large, very golden eyes.

David felt something fuzzy and warm enter his head. Everything around him was melting into the fluffiness of a watercolor painting. He quickly shut his eyes and covered them with his arm, staggering back in a flash of panic. He tripped and plummeted off the platform of the wagon, landing with a thud on the ground. David shook his aching head and looked up.

The woman had risen from her bed and was walking towards him, on all fours. She did not walk on human hands and feet, but great lioness paws, and a long fur-tipped tail swished out behind her. Two violet-black wings opened from her back, as if made from pure midnight. The great mane of hair draped around her, like a shroud, and those glowing golden eyes bore into him like hot branding irons. Her lips pulled back unnaturally towards her ears, baring a predator's teeth, sharp for tearing flesh.

He had read about such a thing as this before, from ancient tales about vicious monsters with the bodies of lions and heads of women. But to see a sphinx in person was nothing like the old philosophers' sketches or artisans' statues that he had seen. Sphinxes were described as man-eaters, who would either strangle their victims with their jaws or simply rip them to pieces and devour them. They were also cunning and deceiving, although sometimes benevolent and noble if they were in the mood. David was hoping this one could be coerced into being the latter. He had never read about sphinxes having a hypnotic power, but it was its teeth and claws that he was focusing on at the moment.

David's shock was trumped by his sense of self-preservation, and his fingers fumbled for his pouch. Fortunately, supernatural hypnosis was not something beyond his knowledge, and his books had warned him on how to guard against it. He drew out the mirror, turning his gaze away from the sphinx and instead looking at her through the mirror's reflection. Even though the shine of her eyes was still apparent in the reflection, it had no effect on him. David was glad that the Greek myth of Perseus, who had used the same tactic against the gorgon Medusa with his shield so her gaze would not turn him into stone, held true in that respect.

"Your little hypnosis won't work on me," David bragged, getting onto his feet and keeping his dagger pointed towards the sphinx, not daring to glance away from her reflection in the mirror.

The sphinx did not seem threatened by this. Instead she shook her mane and inhaled deeply, her chest expanding, and then whispered forth a sweet-smelling scent, a mist of lavender, vanilla and rose that clouded David's face. The scent invaded David's nose and throat, commanding his body and brain to relax, making him feel woozy and happy at the same time. David snapped himself out of it, reaching back into his pouch and pulling out the two small corks. He shoved the corks up his nostrils and breathed through his mouth. He had thought to buy the corks from an apothecary's shop after the night the creature had broken into his room at the inn, remembering the enchanting aroma that had lulled him into false serenity.

The sphinx blinked perplexedly, tilting her head to the side. Then a grin spread across her face. David wrinkled his brow, wondering what the sphinx was smiling about, until he heard a chorus of growls behind him. Turning, David lowered his mirror to see the gypsy men and the dogs, all staring at him. The men frowned at him menacingly, a few of them cracking their knuckles. The dogs bared their teeth and snarled.

He hadn't planned what to do in this situation.

The men pounced at him, taking hold of his arms and pinning him to the ground. When David tried to break free, the dogs bit at his trousers. He couldn't fight back. The weight of the men made him immobile, and his dagger was wrenched from his hands. He could only wriggle madly as his hands and ankles were tied tightly with a coarse rope, and his belt and pouch were stripped of him. They smashed his mirror, and tore the corks from his nose. Then they raised their fists in preparation to knock him senseless.

The sphinx made a soft coo, and the men and dogs immediately stepped away from David. The creature approached the bound boy, her expression gentle but keen. David thrashed about, pulling with all his might to free his hands from the rope, but the men had tied him down superbly. The sphinx looked up at the others, her eyes glowing. The men became drowsy, and they lay down one by one and returned to snoring contentedly.

David held his breath and shut his eyes, refusing to be taken in by the sphinx's spells. He felt one of her strong arms wrap around his waist, her claws digging into his side, and he was dragged along the ground. He was lifted up and set down on something soft. He opened an eye, and found himself inside the sphinx's bowl, with the hypnotic monstrosity settled next to him. The sphinx gazed at him fixedly, but made no sign of her intentions. David continued to struggle against his bindings, even though she spread one feathered wing over him to hold him still.

"You're making a big mistake," David barked. "Nothing you do will make me your slave. The instant

I'm out of these ropes, I'll destroy you and free all these people from your spell. Do you understand me?"

The sphinx merely blew a soothing aroma into his nose. David gagged on the scent, but could not prevent it from taking effect and caressing him into the most blissful sleep he had had in a long time.

CHAPTER TWO

David awoke the next morning to the smell of something delicious. He blinked open his eyes wearily, not remembering where he was at first. He took in his surroundings, and then recalled the events from the previous night. The sphinx was not at his side, but he was still tied up. He craned his neck to look over at the camp. Everyone was having breakfast. There was a large pot cooking over the bonfire, brewing a thick hearty stew. Baskets of fruit and bread were placed near the fire pit, and a jug of milk was being passed around from person to person.

Each gypsy took his or her fair share of food: half a loaf of bread, one or two choices of fruit, and a decent sized bowl of the stew. What was peculiar was that the sphinx was the one serving the stew with a wooden ladle in her paw. The toes of her front paws were more elongated and flexible than those of a typical lion—they were like stubby fingers with claws at the tips. The stew smelled so intoxicating, David was drooling a river. He sighed, realizing that he would probably get no breakfast, or any meal for that matter, until he was willing to give in to the foul animal. He tried again to see if he could wriggle out of his ropes, but his muscles ached too much to make a good effort. He laid his head back against the side of the bronze bowl, his mind racing with thoughts of how he would get out of this mess.

A bowl of stew was placed on the pillow next to him. He looked over at the sphinx, which had approached so quietly he had not noticed. The beast had half of an orange in her teeth, and she laid the fruit on David's lap. The young man looked down at the food, and wondered if the sphinx intended to hand-feed him. She nudged him to turn a little, and then used her claws to cut through the ropes binding his hands. David sat up, rubbing his reddened wrists. The sphinx did nothing to free his ankles, however, and the knots were so strong that David could not untie them.

David took the bowl of stew and slurped it slowly, casting suspicious glances at his host. She just sat there watching him, tilting her head from side to side occasionally. When David finished, he set the bowl down and crossed his arms. The sphinx leaned forward and nudged the orange in his lap.

"I don't want it," David huffed. He picked it up and tossed it at her feet. The sphinx looked down at the fruit, and then glanced over at the others. The caravan folk had finished their breakfast as well, and were now cleaning up camp. She picked the orange up in her teeth and sucked the juice out of it.

Strange, David thought, *for a supposed man-eater to eat fruit. It doesn't look like she touched any of the stew at all. Was she waiting to be sure everyone else got their share first before she had her meal?*

The caravan folk packed up everything quickly but efficiently. Two of the men lifted up the platform and heaved it up back into place, closing the wagon. The sphinx pulled a cord hanging over her nest, opening a small window in the ceiling for light.

"What's going on?" David shouted, hoping that maybe one of the people might tell him. Instead of getting a verbal response, he felt the wagon start to move. "Wait! You can't leave! Let me out of here! Can't any of you hear me? *Por favor! Ayudame!* "

He shouted a bit more, in French, English, and Spanish, but it was no use. The people were under the sphinx's possession. David held his face in his hands, anger and panic shaking him. He couldn't believe that he was being kidnapped, especially right before the start of his apprenticeship! The worst of it was, no one knew he had gone looking for the gypsies, so no one would know what became of him. His parents would start to worry when there would be no letter from him, but it would take them days to realize this, and by then who knew what would become of him?

The sphinx cooed gently to him, curling up at his feet. David was very tempted to lash out and strike the beast. She could at least act like a sphinx should, instead of all this tender torture. The wagon was noticeably crowded, full of baskets of merchandise, performance props, and food. David began to wonder under which category—merchandise, tool or food—the sphinx considered him.

"You can't keep me like this," he barked, more so to vent than to get a response. "There are people who will find out that I am missing. They'll have authorities searching in every city in France. And sooner or later, you will make a mistake and I will escape, and the first thing I will do is …"

He stopped when he realized that the sphinx had not been listening to what he was saying. Her attention was on the necklace of garlic cloves that he was still wearing. She swatted at it gently with her paw, like a kitten playing with a ball of yarn. David rubbed his forehead in irritation. He removed the garlic and threw it at the sphinx, but she only caught it in her teeth and started chewing contentedly on it.

She liked garlic. So much for warding off evil.

The sphinx crept over to David, turned over and lay down on his lap. She laid her head back, exposing her belly and wagging the tip of her tail. David leaned away, recoiling from her as if she were a poisonous serpent. It took him a good minute to realize that the sphinx was asking for her belly to be rubbed.

"No, I'm not scratching you," David said darkly, crossing his arms and slouching into himself. The sphinx looked up at him, making a purring sound in her throat.

David turned his head away. She pawed at his ear, but he flinched away from her. Her long tail flipped up and smacked him in the head like a whip.

"Ow!" David uncrossed his arms to rub his head, but as soon as he did, the sphinx reached up and grabbed his wrist in her paw. She forced his hand down towards her stomach, and did not let go until he moved his fingers in a scratching motion. She grinned and laid her head back again, purring.

David sighed, lightly rubbing the sphinx's stomach as he rested his chin in his other hand.

"Yesterday, I was the next great aspiring architect," David mumbled. "Today, I'm a beast's belly scratcher. Could this possibly get any worse?"

The caravan journeyed a good distance that day, leaving the forested land and entering into wide open plains of golden grass. The caravan stopped at midday to have a quick lunch of fried eggs. After they finished eating, the women went about plucking the feathers from a few reserved ducks that they would cook for dinner. Once again the sphinx ate nothing until everyone else finished. David wondered what she would do if he should decide to skip a meal. Would the sphinx refuse to eat if he refused as well? He couldn't afford to test that theory right now, however. If he was to escape, he needed all the food and energy he could get.

That evening, after they set up camp and consumed a delectable dinner, the caravan folk presented a series of performances to entertain one another—or entertain the sphinx, at any rate. The group sat in a circle while the animals lolled around the camp. The musicians played lively nimble pieces as dancers twirled and laughed around the fire. David was placed next to the sphinx, his legs still bound together, and his waist in the grip of the creature's curved claws. The sphinx watched the entertainers with pure devotion, her eyes wide and bright, bobbing her head to the music.

The young magician that David had seen before performed his few clumsy tricks, which the sphinx enjoyed, revealing her sharp teeth. David rolled his eyes, thinking that she must have seen the boy do the same tricks over and over. Everyone applauded, and it did not sound completely artificial. David was beginning to wonder just how hypnotized these people really were. None of their eyes were glazed over, as he had learned in his books. Maybe rather than any enchantment, they were scared into submission, with the threat that the sphinx could possess them to do something regrettable or horrifying.

A little brown-haired girl sat on the other side of David, and she tugged gently on his sleeve. "Do you do anything?" she asked softly.

Everyone turned and looked at him for an answer. David froze, not expecting to actually be called upon to perform. "I … don't have any talent to entertain, if that's what you mean," he said. "I was never a very good musician—" He cut himself off, swallowing back the remainder of his thought.

The sphinx nudged him so he would turn to her. She stared into his eyes, not with any hypnotic intent, but she seemed to be searching for something. Her paw pressed ever so lightly on his left shoulder and under his chin, which caused David to jerk away, thinking she might claw his throat out. She continued her examination of him by taking hold of his left hand, rubbing her paw pads lightly over his fingertips. She suddenly arose, bounded to her bronze nest, riffling under her pillows. After a moment, she produced a viola and bow. It was polished to a shine, as though it had barely been touched.

David's heart plummeted. Somehow, she had figured out he used to play the viola years ago. Had she guessed that simply from the slight crick in his shoulder from when he had difficulty as a child supporting the viola under his chin, and the calluses on his fingers from years of handling the strings? He had given up the instrument a while ago, and simply looking at the viola made him pale. He glanced over at the other musicians, hoping they would offer to play instead. By the eager way they were looking at him, they clearly wanted to hear what musical gift he might have.

The sphinx returned with the viola, placing it gently into his lap. David stared dully at it. She leaned her head down and bit clean through the ropes on his ankles, fully freeing him.

"Go on, boy. Play us a little tune," one of the musicians shouted.

"No, thank you," David replied, pushing the viola away.

The other caravan folk pressed him to rise and play too. The sphinx got behind him, pushing her paws against his back, thrusting him towards the inside of the circle.

"I said, I don't want to!" David retorted, but the shouts for him to perform crescendoed, and the sphinx shoved him almost violently. With a look of utter disgust on his face, he stood up and walked into the circle. He raised the viola to his chin, tuned it, readied his bow … and lowered it again, his body going rigid.

"I get terrible stage fright," he hissed between his teeth. "I can't play in front of so many people."

Everyone was silent, as some of the gypsies gave each other baffled looks. The sphinx, with a sigh of disappointment, raised a paw as a gesture of dismissal. She patted the ground where David had been sitting, and he promptly sat back down, not caring that the others cast him curious glances. He dropped the viola at the sphinx's feet, not giving it—or her—a second look. The performances carried on, now with two of the gypsy girls displaying a lively dance to the beat of drums, but David's mood was too sour to enjoy any of it.

At some point during the festivities, the sphinx's eyes

glowed, and she breathed a blanket of sweet-smelling serenity over the audience. All the people and animals in the circle began to drift off into a deep sleep, slumping over onto the ground—all except David. The sphinx moved forward to him, sitting squarely at his feet. David gulped, thinking that he was about to be delivered some punishment for having refused to play along. But the sphinx looked up at him as a child looks up at a beloved parent. She picked up the viola in her paws, and offered it to him again.

David threw his gaze back and forth between the viola, and the sphinx's imploring expression. "No, I still don't want to play."

The sphinx pushed the viola at him, cooing at him earnestly.

"When I said I couldn't play in front of so many people, that didn't mean I'd be fine playing it for a private performance. I don't play anymore."

The sphinx frowned in impatience. Now she was hissing at him, and she stood up on her hind legs, puffing out her wings to look bigger and menacing. David instantly got up onto his feet, more confused than scared—even on her hind legs, she was only an inch or two taller than he was. He had the viola in his hands, and glowered at her in indignation.

When he didn't play, she thwacked his legs with her tail.

"Stop that!" David demanded. "I'm tired. I haven't

got the energy to play. Just let me sleep like everyone else."

The sphinx narrowed her eyes, thumping her tail demandingly on the ground.

For Pete's sake, why wasn't he making a run for it? True, running through an open field from a sphinx that could fly and dive down on him did not seem like a good idea, but anything would be worth getting away from being treated like a trained monkey. He held the viola tight in his hand, strangling the neck of it. "Look, I already told you, I'm not your slave. You can't make me do everything you want. I refuse to play for you!"

The sphinx's jaws were well in range to clamp onto David's neck. She did not make a sound, nor made an attempt to hypnotize him. Instead, she tossed her nose in the air and made a snooty snort.

David was so enraged by this display of conceit that he threw the viola on the ground, finishing it off with a powerful stomp of his boot. He then kicked the mangled instrument into the fire.

The sphinx stared into the fire as it devoured her wooden songbird of strings. She sank down slowly onto her haunches, a tiny whimper hanging on her lips. David turned and walked away, away from that cursed camp, away from the caravan, away from that beast. He did not get very far before he heard an enraged snarl behind him. He did not even look back—he took off like a bolt out of a crossbow.

41

David had barely sprinted ten feet before he was rammed to the ground by a heavy pounce from the sphinx. He covered his head, feeling the sphinx's claws tearing at his shirt and pants, all the while she was hissing and growling for blood. Her jaws fastened around the nape of his neck. Her hot breath stung his skin. David squeezed his eyes shut as he waited for his throat to be ripped out.

Suddenly she stopped. She stepped off of him. David remained on the ground for a minute longer before opening his eyes and glancing up. The sphinx was gone. He turned over, and spotted her hidden in the tall grass. She had her wings folded over her head, and she shook terribly. David could hear her soft muffled crying.

There was no text that David had ever read about a sphinx feeling remorse about anything. He was a bit flabbergasted by this.

David got onto his feet, but he did not run. He walked over to the trembling creature, and after a long hesitation placed a hand on her back. A creeping sense of pity seized him before he withdrew his hand. No, he could not let sentimentality get to him. This may be his only opportunity to leave, for the sphinx would not stop him now. He walked over to the front wagon of the caravan train, and unhitched one of the burly white horses from the pulling poles. He took the reins and was just about to mount, when a low moan caressed him from behind. He looked at the sphinx coming up to him. She howled softly, pouring sorrow, shame, and the desire for forgiveness into David's body. He felt tears forming in his eyes.

"No, stop it! I don't want to know how you feel." He angrily rubbed the tears away, and jumped onto the horse. She howled again, and it made David cringe. He kicked the horse, and it began to plod away.

His body jerked as her claw caught him by the pant leg. He looked at her again, straight into her glowing gold eyes. He was not being coerced into sleep, but into that strange state between consciousness and sleep, when people begin to see dreamy thoughts forming in their minds, when their subconscious is wide open but reality has not faded away.

The image of someone he knew, from a long time ago, entered his mind. It was as clear as if she was right in front of him, the same hazel eyes, the warm smile, the slender fingers that would brush strands of mahogany-tinted hair away from her face. Then that someone vanished, like she had all those years ago. The same feelings of abandonment he had felt then resurfaced now.

David was thrust back to full consciousness. The sphinx's prodding of his memories pierced him to his soul. She did not follow after him, but watched him fixedly. She had been searching for a memory to make him know how she was feeling, but her expression showed that even she had not expected the intensity of loneliness and rejection that he had felt from that remembrance.

He turned away. His horse continued into the night.

Something was strange about this terrain. It became more apparent as David pressed on, urging on his stolen horse. Only a few miles back, where the caravan had stopped for the night, it had seemed like regular open plain. But now the further he rode on, night distorted the land around him. A mist settled everywhere, making it hard to see if there was any road or civilization up ahead. All that David could make out was the moon in the sky, but even that ceased to look like the celestial lantern he knew so well. It looked like the distant end to a bleak channel that he kept moving towards, or an unblinking eye watching his every move.

There was a roadside inn about five miles away from the camp, which was inviting to David after the wagon he had been confined to the last few days. He paused, however, wondering if he should continue on, despite his commandeered horse being uncooperative and constantly stopping to graze. This inn was the only one around for many miles from what he could tell. If the sphinx sent her collective after him, they undoubtedly would check here. Plus, David did not have money, and he doubted he could argue his way towards a free night's stay. On the other hand, maybe the innkeeper could barter a night's lodging in exchange for this horse, or could give him directions to the closest town.

As he rode up to the inn, a young stable boy came out to meet him. The boy took the reins from David and led the horse away towards the inn's stables. David couldn't help but notice something seemed unusual about the lad. The boy had said nothing, avoided eye contact with him and had worn no shoes—his feet were mud-caked and his toenails resembled owl talons. David shrugged it off, assuming the boy must be shy—and fairly unhygienic— and he walked through the inn's front door, over which hung a sign, "Poppet's Pub and Inn."

Upon entering, he found the parlor of the inn to be teeming with guests. Groups huddled tightly together at their tables, as if in secretive games of cards. There was a candlelit chandelier hanging overhead, but it cast a dim light down over its shadowy patrons. David instantly noticed the smell—a dank, foul stench that reminded him of bad eggs and stale rotted meat. He coughed, and his face wrinkled as the taste of that stench coated the inside of his mouth.

His cough resonated through the room. It was quiet enough to hear a mouse breathing at the far end of the hall. The patrons did not notice, however, and they remained huddled together without acknowledging the newcomer in the doorway.

David cleared his throat, hoping he could contain his coughing to speak. "Excuse me, might one of you tell me where I could find the keeper of this inn?"

His voice withered into silence when no one looked up to regard him. Maybe he had unwittingly interrupted a private dinner party, and they were irritated with him. Everyone was dressed finely enough, in satin gowns and waistcoats, although their apparel looked like they could stand a good washing and mending. There was no music, no decorations, and nothing to indicate that there was any merrymaking. The only party décor were the large porcelain punch bowls sitting on each table, to which all the people leaned in close. David was extremely parched, and he approached one of the tables.

"Please, I have just been through a terrible ordeal, and I am so thirsty. I hope you don't mind if I share in your drink?" he asked one of the lady patrons wearing a tattered brown dress. She kept her head down, staring at the bowl, not speaking a word. David thought to himself that she needed to tend to her hair, which was a matted, wild mess hanging like dead vines around her face. As a matter of fact, everyone had the same wild, straggly tresses trailing from their heads, even the men.

When he looked into the punchbowl, he could see it was full of a deep, red wine. But it didn't smell like wine. It was also thicker than wine. And chucks of meat and skin were floating in it.

David gasped in horror, his lungs unable to pump any air. He let out a bark in panic as the lady in the brown dress lashed out with her hand and grabbed his arm. The instant she touched him, he felt his blood chill, the warmth being drained from his body. Her grasp was a crushing vice, and David could not escape her grip. Her hands were not made of flesh, but segmented pieces of splintered wood, and it was snagging his skin. With all his strength, he pulled back to get free of her, and with a loud crack, he broke free—or, more accurately, he broke her hand clean off of her wrist. The wooden hand kept clinging to him until he shook it off so violently, it flew across the room, smacking into a far wall.

David for the first time took a good, hard look at the faces around him. He had thought that the poor lighting of the room had made their features dark and indistinct, but now he could see otherwise. Rows upon rows of gaunt faces, with black empty eyes, turned to stare at David. The hair on their heads was driven into their scalps in chunks, the way one digs a fistful of straw into a patch of mud. Their mouths were void of emotion—no smiles or grimaces—although some had crooked teeth protruding from their lipless gums. David also could see now that their faces were not made of skin and flesh, but paint and clay.

Dolls. Dolls that were alive. Dolls that craved blood.

The guests were standing up, one by one, in stiff, jerking movements that caused their bodies to creak and snap and groan. Slowly, twitchingly, desperately, they extended their wooden hands towards David, their stiff feet shuffling through the dust, grime, and sticky stains coating the floor.

If David's stories of vampires and demons had taught him anything, such monsters always preferred fresh, warm blood to stale, cold blood. He turned to run out the door, only to find that the door was now gone—only blank wall was behind him.

Blast it! This whole place was a trap!

He furiously scanned the room for a window or means of escape, but the dolls were closing in fast. *I should have just played that stupid viola!*

He found a sharp piece of broken bone on the floor nearby, and made a mad dash for it. The dolls were on him, grasping at his clothes and searching for his flesh. Their rotten teeth—mismatched collections of human teeth, animal fangs, shards of glass and chipped stone— were bared in ravenous hunger. David slashed out at them with the bone, but realized this did little to faze them.

David kicked one of the dolls straight in the chest, sending it staggering back, but not deterring it as it resumed its pursuit. Running with all his speed, David leapt onto one of the tables and made a strong jump towards the chandelier, which he just managed to grab a hold on. He tried to climb up higher onto it, but the rafter started to give way under his additional weight.

He could feel the dolls below snapping at his feet with their teeth, clutching at his boots with their splintered hands and yanking down.

Something came straight through the wall of the inn, tearing through it like paper. Big black wings wrapped around David, pulling him off the chandelier and high overhead, breaking through the sheet-thin roof. The dolls below were enraged, clacking their teeth and tearing out their own hair in starving anguish. David heard a female voice speaking something in an unusual tongue. As he clung to his rescuer, hovering in the air, he recognized the language as Latin, for he had studied it in school. The dialect was very heavy, bestial in tone, but he managed to decipher some of the words ...

Away ... home ... this ... one... mine ... banish ... you ...

Then the floor of the inn broke away, like ice flows in the presence of heat, and the blood-drinkers tumbled down into darkness, and the inn itself was sucked down in a whirlpool of blood and bone ...

David blacked out.

CHAPTER THREE

"You all right there, boyo?"

David awoke to the sound of wheels rumbling along the ground. He slowly opened his eyes to a room lighted by a lantern. He was inside one of the moving caravan wagons. All along the walls hung rows of rabbits, squirrels, ducks and geese, the spoils of the hunt and several nights' dinners for the caravan. The room was saturated with the odors of meat and fur. The Scottish juggler was sitting next to him, smoking a long pipe. He had a snide smirk plastered on his face.

"You took my best puller. It's a pain on the other horses to pull the train without that one," he spat. "Fortunately the mistress got him back safe and sound, along with you."

David blinked, and sat up on the straw mattress. "I'm sorry for taking the horse, Señor …?"

"Gullin. No Señor, or Mister, or none of that."

"Now that one of you has decided to talk to me, Gullin, maybe I won't have to act so rudely. I don't suppose you could drop me off at the next town."

Gullin chuckled. "Next town isn't going to be for

a while now. Here, drink up." He handed David a clay stein. David welcomed the drink gladly, as he was very thirsty. He coughed at the potency of the unexpected liquor, having assumed it would be water.

The drink jostled something in his brain, and he recalled the events of the previous night. "What on earth happened? There was an inn, and there were all these man-sized dolls, living walking dolls! I think they wanted to drink my blood—"

"Ah, the Jenglots. Nasty buggers. They don't actually 'drink' blood. They drink up its warmth until the victim is stone-cold dead. They need the warmth to stay alive. And the younger the blood, the better. " Gullin stood up and moved to the other side of the wagon, where he rummaged through a wooden chest. "It's a problem once you start crossing through the Curtain. You can never be quite sure what gates to the unknown you might stumble through when you're alone out here. Luckily the mistress knows how to handle Jenglots and the like. This should help calm the mind a bit." He took a small leather pouch out of the chest. He walked back over and gave it to David. "A secret family remedy for the spooks."

David looked into the pouch, finding it full of pellets that smelled of sage, but he thought better of eating any of them, so he pocketed the bag. "What do you mean, 'crossing through the Curtain'? I've never heard of a territory called that in these parts."

"Not surprising. Most folks wouldn't have heard it. You can call it the Veil, or the Gates, or whatever you please. Let's just say, you best stay with the group. You're not familiar with what this place can do."

The younger man took a good look at his surroundings. "I suppose you're going to give me some kind of punishment for having run away. *She* would probably be more than happy for you to do so."

The juggler grimaced. "She didn't eat a bite this morning, on account of you. She's been sick as a dog. If she starves to death, I'll smash your head against the first rock I find."

David knotted his eyebrows. "You wouldn't be happy to be free of her possession?"

Gullin gave him a long hard look. "Boy, you obviously don't understand a blasted thing." He sat back in a simple wooden chair, bouncing to the rhythm of the wagon's movement.

"Do you honestly believe you are not under her control?" David inquired.

"The mistress doesn't work that way."

"She enchants you people to do her bidding. Don't you even remember how she possessed you and the others to tie me up the other night?"

Gullin glared at him. "You were the one who woke us up with your bumbling, and you were holding a dagger up at the mistress. You should be thanking her. If she hadn't stopped us, we would've beaten you to a pulp."

David scratched his head. "But … she hypnotizes you all to sleep. I saw it."

"Nothing wrong with sleep when you need it." Gullin stretched his arms and neck.

"Is that a real Master Huntsmen's crest on your arm?" David asked, pointing at the tattooed symbol. "Just who are you, anyway?"

The Scotsman sighed. He took the stein back from David and took a swig from it. "Now you want me to be getting personal. Boyo, I was a Huntsman—a very special class of the brotherhood, tells you how I know all about this side of the Curtain—" he gestured around himself with a broad sweep of his arm, "but it ain't all you think it is. Frankly, it doesn't provide steady income, 'specially with monsters and the fairy tale types getting fewer and fewer. Truth is, the day I was on my last coin and about ready to call it quits with it all, this caravan came rolling by. I thought it might need a good pair of arms, and they seemed to be getting good money, so I asked to join up with it."

"You joined on your free will? Did you know about *her*?"

"No, not at first, and I was a bit surprised, I can tell you. But the mistress is good. Makes sure we all have plenty to eat, treats us fairly, lets us spend the money we make. We're like family. " He took another long drink.

"But … she abducts people for her caravan. She kidnapped me! And she tried to rob me."

Gullin raised an eyebrow at him.

"She did!" David insisted. "She broke into my room at the inn, and then I scared her off, but she dropped my purse on the floor."

"Ay, that." Gullin sighed. "Now an apology does need to be given, but not from the mistress. I'm afraid bad habits die hard for some of us. Isabella, the girl who gave you that dagger, was a pickpocket since she was wee. Only way she could survive on the streets. The mistress has been trying to break her of the habit, but Izzy couldn't help herself when it was so easy for the taking. The mistress was trying to return your purse to you before you realized you'd been pilfered."

David was about to argue that he had his purse with him the whole time, but it dawned on him that he hadn't checked his pockets after his participation in the juggling act. He had gone straight to his room at the inn afterwards, so he hadn't even thought of his purse before going to bed. Even if it were true the sphinx was only returning the purse, he noted, "Maybe, but she was still thinking about eating me. Why else would she be sniffing at me while I was sleeping?"

"Mibbae you smell funny."

David furrowed his eyebrows, finding irony that the Scotsman thought *he* was the one who smelled funny. "So, you say you people are here because you want to work for this … this creature—"

"The mistress," Gullin corrected him sharply.

"Yes, her," David replied holding up his hands in defense. "But *I* don't want to be. If she isn't the kind to keep prisoners, then why am I one?"

Gullin sighed. "There are some rules about what to do with folks who 'see the unseen,' so to speak. Those who live on the other side of the Curtain went there to remain a secret, to live peacefully without humans trying to muck it up. You have to prove you're good at keeping the knowledge secret, since if you went blabbing about it to everyone, it would cause a good deal of trouble. Can't let you go starting up a panic, can we?"

David shook his head. "But no one where I come from believes the stories I tell. If I went back and told them I was kidnapped by a sphinx, who is going to believe me?"

The man shrugged. "Mibbae you're here for another reason."

David narrowed his eyes. "Such as?"

"The mistress's wise. She might be wanting to teach you something. Her kind work in mysterious ways. Sphinxes have made poor men into kings, and been advisors to the greatest minds. Betcha didn't know that, boyo."

Actually, David had read a book or two that had said as much, but those were from myths. Plus, the tale of the sphinx in Greece who had led a man to become king also led to that king gouging out his own eyes. "How do you know she wants to teach me something?"

"Mibbae she does, mibbae she doesn't. She might just want you around for another reason."

"Like … food?"

Gullin laughed again. "Hardly. Let's just say, I ain't seen the mistress take a liking to anyone like she has to you in a long time. She might be feeling a bit lonely."

"Lonely? She has all of you. Your 'family,' as you put it."

"That's not the kind of 'lonely' I'm talking about. You can be surrounded by people and still be lonely. Sometimes, you need just the right person around. You understand?"

David quickly changed the subject. "So, you're telling me none of you are really under her enchantment?"

"Well, she had to give some of the others the glowin' eye to keep them calm—you know, they get antsy around things they don't understand. But most of us, we don't cause trouble. We like the three meals a day."

"And none of you explained this to me earlier because …?"

"The mistress doesn't like us talking to a new member unless she's sure he's going to be part of the group. She don't want us getting too attached if the guy's not sticking around."

"You think I'm going to stay?"

Gullin gave him a smirk. "That's all up to the mistress now, ain't it?"

The sphinx had not come out of her wagon even into the afternoon. When one of the gypsies peeked in to bring her herbal tea made from the sphinx's favorite flowers, the creature stayed curled up in her nest and would not eat. The caravan folk worried that her illness was severe and they should make her some stronger medicine, but Gullin had another theory.

"She ain't been acting right since she saved you from those Jenglots," Gullin snarled at David as he grabbed him by the collar and shoved him towards the sphinx's wagon. "You talk to the mistress," he ordered. "Or I'll wring your scrawny neck."

David sighed, not sure how he was actually supposed to "talk" to her. According to myth, sphinxes were capable of human speech, and he was sure that she had spoken to the Jenglots. He approached the wagon and tapped on the side. "Hello in there. It's me, David."

No reply. David cleared his throat, irked that all the gypsies were staring at him. "I ... I wanted to be sure that you're well." He paused. "May I see you?"

A soft murr came from inside. David and another man took hold of the wagon's side and carefully lowered it open. The sphinx lifted her head, casting her gaze deep into David's eyes. She arose slowly, her legs and wings a little stiff, and ambled out of the nest over to him. Her face was pale, her hair matted, her limbs seemed scrawnier, but more noticeably her normally healthy lips were dried and cracked. She more resembled a mangy alley cat than a majestic lioness. She moaned softly.

David wondered if maybe her encounter with the Jenglots had made her ill. He leaned in close, hoping the others would not hear. "I'm sorry that you are sick. You didn't have to save me from the Jenglots, but you did. Thank you, for that."

She smiled weakly.

"I want to make sure you get better. But I'm only staying until we get to the next town. Then I'm gone. Is that clear?" David said this knowing the sphinx would not respond, but he said it loud enough so the caravan folk would also hear.

With her paw, the sphinx picked up an orange from one of the food baskets, and held it up to David. He took the fruit, peeled it and took a bite. He pulled a slice from it and gave it to her. She hesitated in taking it, but then she bit down on it and sucked out the juice. She did not finish the fruit until he was done eating.

After the caravan train rolled across the fields, David and the sphinx sat in the bronze nest, sharing the herbal tea. Then she was treated to another nice, however reluctantly given, belly rub.

That night, David found himself staring out onto a shimmering sapphire ocean. He was lying on a grassy shore under a small birch tree, its leaves green and trimmed in gold. A gentle wind carried fresh fragrances of grass, flowers, and everything pure. He was not sure how he had come to be there, or where "there" even was, but he felt such peace that his whereabouts did not matter.

With him was a woman. He did not know how long she had been there before he noticed her, but she stood patiently, smiling. As she approached, he realized it was the sphinx, only completely human. Her paws were finely shaped hands and feet. She had no tail, and no wings. Her face was different too, particularly the eyes that were now an inviting emerald green. She was draped in a white dress fitted to her sleek shape.

David took a long look at the woman, before giving her a gentle smile. "Hello," was all he could think to say.

She walked to him, and sat down at his side. She gazed deeply into his eyes, and as David gazed back, he could make out that the green of her eyes had a ring of gold around them, and the gold glimmered like sunlight passing through crystal.

"How did I get here?" he inquired.

You brought yourself here. This is your ideal place.

Her voice was crisp and clear, but she had not moved her lips to reply. The voice was inside David's head.

He sat up quickly, frightened by how real this dream was, and of what the sphinx might be doing to him while he was distracted by this illusion.

She gently placed a hand on his shoulder and pushed him back down. *There is no need to be worried. It is time for us to know each other better. I want to talk.*

"Talk is fine … just please don't … uh … you're not doing anything strange while I'm sleeping, are you?"

No, you need not fear. I chose this form because it calms humans and makes them feel less intimidated.

"Ah." A question popped into his mind, but the sphinx answered it before he could verbally ask.

Yes, a sphinx is normally able to speak as you humans do. But time has changed things. This is the only way I can communicate without … risking my health.

"Risking your health? How—"

She sharply cut him off. *I don't wish to discuss it.* Her tone softened again as she said, *I wish to discuss you. To know who you are, what you like, what you are thinking.*

David gave the woman another good look-over. "The way you look reminds me of someone I knew once, back in Cervera. But that was a long time ago. She went far away, and I never heard from her again. She probably doesn't remember me now, I don't think." He dismissed the memory quickly, reburying it in his past.

You humans make your lives so sad sometimes, because of fear.

"I don't see why you want to 'talk' like this. I take it you could just read my mind and know everything about me that you want to know?"

60

Perhaps. But there's no trust in that. I want you to trust me, David.

"Why?"

Because I want you to stay with me. I cannot force you to remain here, for you are more strong-minded than most. I'm using my abilities at their highest extent to create this reality for you.

David sat up again, brushing his fingers through the grass. "But it's not real. It's just an illusion."

What is real is only what you can understand with your five senses. But if I breathe life into what you see, and hear, and taste, and touch ... She placed a hand on his knee. *And smell...* She blew a soft breeze of lilac towards him. *Then this place is just as real as any other.*

David stared into her eyes. "But I know it's not real."

Why is that so important? Isn't this your ideal place? Do you not like my appearance?

The last sentence she said startled him. Did she want him to think she was beautiful? "It doesn't matter. It's simply knowing. It's knowing that outside all these beautiful things, I'm still prisoner to an animal who has me under her spell. It's knowing that I'm not free."

I gave you the chance to be free of me. You came back.

"I had to! I don't have a choice when I'm out in the middle of nowhere, being attacked by bloodthirsty puppets, and my only way of getting back to civilization is to ride this nightmare train." David stood up and walked a few feet away.

Am I so awful to you, David? he heard her ask. He cringed slightly as she said his name. He couldn't help but think it was the loveliest way he had ever heard his name spoken.

"It doesn't seem fair you should know my name, and I don't know yours," he noted.

You know my name. I am a Sphinx.

"I mean, your real name, not your species. You don't call me Human, after all."

I was never given a name of that type. I have always been a Sphinx.

"Then what do others call you? Surely your family gave you a name."

No. My earliest ancestor was born of the Typhoon and the Great Drakaina. I and my kind have always been called the creatures that we are. What would you call me?

He stood silently for a while.

"I want to wake up now," he replied.

The caravan train came to a sudden halt.

David woke up abruptly as the wagon came to a stop. The sphinx was curled up next to him, and she slowly opened her eyes. She stretched her muscles and yawned, her lips pulling back again in that wide frightening gape. David still had not gotten used to it. Yet she did look much better, her skin having returned to its golden hue and her lips no longer cracked. She sighed contentedly.

David pressed his ear to the wall of the wagon. He heard the gypsies scurrying around outside, and the sound of instruments being tuned.

"What are they up to out there?" he wondered. He unlatched the hooks holding the wagon wall closed. He paused, glancing back at the sphinx. She smiled at him, and motioned with her paw that he could go outside.

David lowered the wall and stepped outside. The gypsies were donning their performance outfits, tuning their instruments and readying their wares. Gullin was already practicing a warm-up routine with his torches, when he spotted David.

"Hey there, boyo! Time for another day's work. Here, make yourself useful." Gullin picked up an empty bucket and tossed it at David. "Think you can fetch a little water?"

David was piqued, as he had never consented to be Gullin's lackey. Yet there wasn't much else to do, and it did give him a reason to have some time away from the sphinx. It then dawned on him that there was no source of water nearby. In fact, nothing was nearby. Looking around, a great enclosure of cloudy whiteness surrounded them, and the ground beneath them was flat, grassless earth. He felt like he was in the middle of a giant wad of cotton.

"What water?" he demanded to know.

"Just walk a ways off there," Gullin replied, pointing towards the fog. "But not too far. Don't want you getting lost again."

With a sigh, David walked a few paces, finding that even in the short distance he traveled, the caravan was already fading from view. He walked a little farther, but nothing changed. He paused, remembering how it had been a similar fog that had led him to the Jenglots' trap, and he certainly didn't want to stumble upon anything else by himself. He turned around and went back.

He walked over to the juggler. "Gullin, I don't feel so—"

"Thanks," Gullin replied, taking the bucket back, which was now full of crystal clean water. "Just in case anything goes wrong with my act, be ready to douse me, will you?"

David gawked at the full bucket. "But ... how ... I didn't see any ..."

Gullin snickered. "That ain't the most surprising thing you're going to see tonight, boyo."

The same three painted wagons that the gypsies had taken into Orléans for their public performance were hitched up to the white horses, and the gypsy parade began through the fog. David hesitated, wondering whether to follow them or stay behind with the rest of the caravan train. He did wonder exactly where the procession was going, and while the thought of whatever lay ahead in the fog worried him, he was more worried about being alone with the sphinx. This, however, turned out not to be an issue, for the sphinx had left her nest and had come to stand next to him. She stood up on her hind legs, but not in the awkward way dogs or cats might do it, but naturally like a human. A white skirt wrap was tied around her waist to match her chest scarf, adding to the illusion of her seeming more human than animal. She curled her tail around David's waist and led him along, tailing after the parade.

She's coming too? He wondered silently. *In what kind of place are we that she is not afraid of revealing herself?*

The fog thickened, so much so that David eventually could not see the train of wagons or people in front of them. He could barely see his hand in front of his face. But the sphinx kept leading him on unwaveringly. The same deathly quiet he had experienced in The Poppet's Pub was around him. He gulped, deciding to fill the silence a bit.

"You know, I've been trying to think of a name for you," he said.

The sphinx said nothing.

"Would you like a name?"

Her tail squeezed his waist a little, which David took to mean yes.

"Well, I was thinking … I heard you like Egyptian flowers, which I guess makes sense since I've read a few stories about sphinxes that lived in Egypt. There's a flower that grows in Egypt called an acacia, and it can be golden in color like you are. I think Acacia would be a good name for you."

The sphinx was quiet for a minute, but then she

nuzzled her head on his shoulder and purred softly.

He took that to mean she liked it.

The fog suddenly parted, and a waterfall of glimmering multicolored lights rose before them. There were soft, tinkling voices all around, like children laughing and singing. Fuzzy orbs of light floated through the air, alighting on each person's head or nose. One gentle green light kissed David's cheek, and he instinctively swatted at it. Acacia grabbed his hand and gave him a stern look, shaking her head.

"What are they?" he asked, even though he knew she couldn't give him a direct answer.

Gullin shouted over the answer to him. "They are here to welcome us and bring us to our host for the evening," he replied. "This is your first time seeing Will O' Wisps, isn't it?"

Will O' Wisps? The fairy fires from folklore? David couldn't believe his eyes. So this is what Gullin had been talking about, "crossing through the Curtain." Acacia, being a magical creature, must have the ability to go back and forth between the human world and the supernatural worlds.

As the gypsies marched on, the floating lights swirled around them happily, as if wanting to be part of the show. David recalled what he had read about Will O' Wisps, that they mysteriously appeared over marshes or bogs at night, for they had an attraction for water. But there was no water here—

Except for the clear blue water they were now walking on.

He hadn't even realized it until he looked down. There was no more earth beneath them, just water as far down as he could see. But the water did not even make his boots wet, and the wagons rolled over the rippling sea as surely as if it were solid ground. David, although a perfectly fine swimmer, found himself clinging tighter onto Acacia as he stared down at the water, wondering if at any second he would plummet right down into the icy depths.

The sphinx chuckled at his anxiety. She nuzzled his cheek, as if to tell him not to worry.

"Just who is our host for the evening?" David called out to Gullin. "Some kind of sea creature?"

"The mistress never misses a chance to see her sisters," Gullin replied, "and it's the night of the Sea Song Festival. It's good for us. We get paid well at these events."

Sisters? Acacia had sisters? He looked at her. "More sphinxes, like you?"

Acacia shook her head, but grinned. She cooed a little melody, gentle like a breeze, and fluttered her wings a little.

David figured this was some kind of riddle, another famous sphinx trait. Singing … wings … was she indicating some kind of bird? These must be sisters in the figurative sense. He found it odd that the gypsies would perform for birds …

That's when he heard actual singing, far off in the distance. A small island was appearing before them, rising out of the water in a wash of greens and blues. Great trees, with brightly blooming flowers, sprouted up all around the island's shores. A stone structure was peaking above the treetops, resembling something like a cross between a mansion and a mountain. But the island's beauty paled in comparison to its symphony. The singing was gorgeous, like something out of a dream.

He knew then that he was hearing the song of sirens.

CHAPTER FOUR

"Welcome, Sister, and to your family." An ochre-skinned woman with the avian traits of an ibis greeted the caravan as it arrived on the island's shore. The siren was more bird than woman, long in neck and slender in body, with silken red feathers sprouting from head to clawed toe. Two other sirens stood behind her, one with the graceful curves and ivory-white down of a swan, and a darker-skinned female with the blade-sharp sleekness and steel-blue plumage of a heron.

Acacia greeted her siren sisters with a bow of the head and a smile. The first siren turned to David. "You are new to us. What is your name?"

The young man was too distracted to answer. His surroundings were beyond his imagination, full of color and light and all the creatures he had learned about in his tomes of myth and legend. Not just the Grecian ones, but Celtic fairy folk, mystic animals of the far East, and he even spotted what appeared to be an elfish dwarf wearing clothing of Norse origin. He snapped to attention and focused on his host. "I am David Sandoval."

"Welcome, David. I am Agalope, and my sisters are Molpe and Thelxepeia. I see our Sister Sphinx admires you very much."

Acacia frowned, making a sharp hiss.

Agalope only giggled. "She is sensitive around us. I forget. Be at ease tonight. You are an esteemed guest in our home."

There was a question burning in David's mind, and he could not help but ask. "I've read a story about sirens, about how ... well, when sailors come to your island to hear your singing ... and they ... well, how can I put this tactfully—"

"Die?"

David tightened his lips. "Yes, that."

The sirens did not seem offended by the inquiry. Molpe answered the question. "Not all sirens are sensible. There are those who find humor in deceiving and hurting humans, but such folly always leads to misfortune. You have no reason to fear any ill intent from us."

"But do you know what I have been waiting for, Sister?" Thelxepeia said, addressing Acacia. "The Teumessian is being such a pest again. I don't know why we even invite him to our festivals anymore."

"He invites himself, Sister," Molpe corrected.

"Well, anyway, someone needs to remind him he's to watch his tongue," Thelxepeia continued. "I know you'll put him in his place, Sister Sphinx." The siren looked into the sphinx's eye, and made a surprised expression. "Oh my, do you have a name now? I had no idea. But I see it, right there, that little glint in your eye. What is it?"

The sphinx looked at David with a smile. She nudged him. David was a little taken aback, but he replied, "Acacia."

"Acacia, how lovely. Appropriate, too. A beautiful flower that has thorns."

David hadn't even thought of that. The floral name Acacia did derive from the plant having large thorns.

Acacia smiled revealing her two rows of sharp teeth.

The Teumessian was nothing like what David had expected. Molpe quickly briefed him that the Teumessian was a descendent of one of the children of the Great Drakaina, the dragon mother who birthed nearly every legendary monster in Greece. David remembered that Acacia, in his dream, had said her earliest ancestor was born of a Drakaina, and he wondered if there was some distant relation between her and this unwelcome guest. Was the Teumessian much like a sphinx himself, or perhaps more reptilian as the name drakaina implied?

A narrow man, whose every facial feature was as sharp as a fresh blade, was seated at a lavishly decorated table, with two beautiful nymphs seated on each side of him. He was dressed in the highest fashion of the time from David's human world, with fine leather shoes, a maroon-red suit and a gold chain laced across his velvet vest. His hair was a fiery orange gold, and his eyes were the same bright orange. Most notably, he had a large fox's tail wrapped around his waist. David at first thought this was an odd accessory, until the tail flicked momentarily, indicating that it was in fact a rear appendage.

"Ah, my dear cousin and her little entourage of peasants have arrived," the fox-tailed man noted dryly. "How quaint. Say, who is your new arm decoration?" He grinned at David with the same warmth a hawk would give to a rabbit.

David hesitated before he introduced himself. "David Sandoval."

"David. How droll." The Teumessian said this unimpressed. "You seem rather dumb, but I could stand to have someone around for a little 'man' talk. Allow me to introduce myself, since your mistress is incapable of formally presenting me ... or anyone for that matter."

Acacia curled her lip at him.

"I am Nicolas Canidae Vulpini. I am also called the Teumessian, but you may call me Nico. Or Sublime, as many do," he joked, casting a glance at one of the nymphs beside him and tickling her under her chin. The nymph giggled childishly.

Acacia rolled her eyes. She mumbled one short word in her cryptic Latin, but even this seemed to cause her difficulty. David did not catch what the word was, but it must have been condescending, because Nico's smile dropped.

"It's a shame you have such a disabled tongue. I almost miss your clever remarks," he replied coolly. "Although, I suppose there are downsides to being too clever. It can leave one lonely in a world full of idiots. Speaking of lonely—David, do you know the story of the Sphinx lineage? It's been passed down in the family for generations."

Acacia's claws pinched into David's skin. She snarled at Nico.

"The first true sphinx, the winged purebred, was the only one of her kind born," Nico continued, oblivious to Acacia's irritation. "A bit hard to reproduce when there's only one of you, isn't it? The first sphinx spent her time plaguing the people of a populace city, devouring any traveler who couldn't answer her riddle—frankly, a rather outdated, silly riddle, but I guess it's a challenge for the *human* brain.

"As you may have read in some poorly written book, a man came along one day and answered the sphinx's riddle. She was so distraught at her defeat, she cast herself off a cliff and fell to her death, and the city rewarded the man by making him king. But then, if that were all true, how do you explain her?" Nico made a careless wave at Acacia. "No, not quite the correct tale. If it hasn't been made clear to you yet, sphinxes tend to be … lovelorn.

And when you're the only one of your species, you may become … desperate for affection."

Acacia's snarl had now developed into a full menacing growl. David winced as her claws dug deeper into his arm.

"The truth is, the sphinx gave that idiot Oedipus the answer, so he could tell the people of Thebes that he had solved the riddle and defeated the beast, and they would make him king. It was her token of love, because all she wanted was for him to be happy." Nico scrunched up his face, as if he had just swallowed a piece of rotten fruit. "So the man became famous, remembered in timeless lore, and in return, he helped the sphinx fake her death and escape from Greece. Eventually she settled in the deserts of Egypt, rumored to have once been a home to a tribe of male lion-men, Nature's prototype of sphinxes perhaps—but she forever pined for that human, like a lovesick fool."

Acacia lunged out with her paws, narrowly missing Nico's face by a hair's breadth, and slammed her claws down on the table. She pulled back, leaving deep gouges in the tabletop. She regained her composure, standing up straight and staring coldly at her cousin.

"That's enough," Agalope said. "This is a sacred festival. I will not allow this sort of hostility in our home. Watch your mouth, Teumessian."

Nico yawned nonchalantly. "I can't help it if she's so touchy." He looked back at David. "That was more for your benefit. Fair warning, is all. Cousin ..." He looked into Acacia's eyes, and saw in them something he had never seen before. It was a subtle change, a soulful spark that those of the Drakaina bloodline could obtain only one way. He wrinkled his nose. "Ugh, you let the boy give you a name? Predictable. How about a short game of riddles? I've been anxious for another round, to give you a chance to best me this time. If, of course, you have the stamina for it."

David thought back to what Acacia had said in his dream, that she was unable to communicate normally without "risking her health." It must have accounted for why she got sick after speaking her banishing spell to the Jenglots. He wondered what the reason was behind it—was she under a curse? Had sphinxes devolved so much that it was a strain on their minds and bodies to speak? Whatever the reason, the Teumessian was exploiting the fact that she could not speak and was taunting her. Hopefully Acacia could see through him and wouldn't give in to the ridicule.

The sphinx sat down at the table. By the look on her face, she was perfectly willing to a contest of riddles. She took a deep breath, and remained perfectly relaxed.

"Bravo, Cousin. Such bravery." Nico leaned his elbows on the table. "But none of that 'what walks on four legs, then two then three' nonsense. That's pathetic."

The war of wits commenced. The two opponents batted riddles back and forth, Acacia posing hers as concisely as she could in soft-spoken Latin, and Nico delivering long-winded conundrums, relishing in the sound of his own voice. Both seeming equally matched in intellect. A small crowd of guests began to gather, and David figured this must be a long standing rivalry in the family to attract such attention. But he could see, gradually, that it was getting more difficult for Acacia to continue. She was getting pale again, sweat beading on her forehead. He wanted to tell her this wasn't necessary, that it was ridiculous to suffer over a stupid game. The deadly glint in her eye, however, warned him not to interfere.

On his fourteenth turn, the Teumessian stated, "A man walks into a tavern and asks the owner for a drink of water. The owner instead draws out and points a knife at the man's face. The man thanks the tavern owner and leaves. Why?"

The sphinx furrowed her eyebrows, and bit her lips. There was a tension hanging in the air, as the other guests waited in anticipation. Acacia tapped her claws on the table as she pondered.

David put a hand to his mouth and made a "hic" sound.

Nico frowned, glaring at him.

David cleared his throat, and made another "hic" sound.

This time Acacia looked over at him curiously. Recognition spread over her face, and she grinned. She looked back at Nico and answered, "*Singultare*." Hiccups.

The guests around them responded simultaneously, "Ahhh."

"That's not fair! The human gave it away," Nico protested.

"I didn't hear him say anything," Thelxepeia said.

"Neither did I," Molpe agreed.

The guests murmured amongst one another. Acacia narrowed her eyes at Nico, but she was smirking. Nico wrinkled his nose again, but calmly replied, "You seem to think you have a knack for this sort of thing, David. I don't suppose you are as good at asking riddles as you are at ruining them?"

David put a finger to his chin as he thought. "Well, I do have one I think is pretty good. But it may be too simple for the likes of you."

Nico knew a dare when he heard one. "Please, by all means, share your simple riddle."

David took a breath—while noting the curious although skeptical look from Acacia—and spoke:

"I save the lives of kings and heroes, if they heed me.

I save the tongues of knaves and charlatans, if they know me.

I turn masters into servants, and fools into wise men.

I bring idols down from their thrones."

Nico pursed his lips, and chuckled. "Did you write that one yourself?" he asked in a manner meaning, *How cute, the boy thinks he's actually intelligent.*

David smiled awkwardly.

The Teumessian shook his head, picking up a wine glass from the table and sipped from it. "Poorly constructed. It's mediocre, at best. You practically give away the answer in the riddle itself."

"Then you must know what it is," David replied.

Nico's smile morphed into a grimace. His orange eyes darkened. "What makes you think you can talk to me like that?"

The boy and the fox-man stared down one another, until David gave him a wry grin of triumph.

Nico slammed his glass down on the table, nearly shattering it. "This is ridiculous. Why do we allow her to bring her humans here? It's degrading and embarrassing, like bringing in a parade of rodents. Now *this* one thinks just because he's her dear favorite, he's worth a lick of salt? Leave the pets at home next time, Cousin, and have a shred of dignity."

Acacia clasped her paws together on the table, and gave him a look that said, *Do you give up?*

Nico shrunk back into his seat, crossing his arms. He remained silent.

"It would seem the Teumessian is stumped," Agalope commented. "But I certainly am curious to know the answer."

"Humility," David responded, "Although, I suppose it was a little unfair to pose that riddle to you, Nico— given that you don't know what humility is."

Acacia tried to muffle her snickering beneath her paw.

After the festivities, the sirens led the caravan's horses to a stable used specifically for the guests' steeds. They offered the gypsies lodging for the night at one of their "nests," which was a lush lagoon surrounded by tall marble columns and finely crafted statues. The water led into a wide-mouthed cave, set up with accommodation much like any of the hotels David would have stayed in back in his own world. As soon as camp was set up along the rim of the lagoon, the caravan folk jumped into the water to bathe. Modesty was apparently not an issue among these people, although the women and children gathered at one spot of the lagoon while the men gathered at another—there was no effort to hide anything.

David opted not to bathe. He lay down on shore, gazing up at the night sky. The faint smells of the women's milk soaps wafted in the air. He heard the laughter of the children as they played in the water. He looked over, watching the boys and girls playing with Acacia as she swam seamlessly across the lagoon's pool. She was as agile and graceful as a fish, her wings spread out like two great fins. She was looking better, although she still moved about carefully, taking time to recover from the riddle match.

"What's the matter with you, boy?" Gullin climbed out of the water and walked up to him. Fortunately, the man still had on his trousers. He had only waded in to splash water on his torso. "Don't want any of the ladies getting a peek?"

"It's not that. It's crowded in there right now."

Gullin grinned, sitting down. "You're a shy one. Too shy. You never join in on the fun."

David had discovered that Gullin was prepared to talk about anything, from the lightly amusing to the bluntly vulgar to the cleverly humorous, but no matter how many times or in what manner David inquired, Gullin would not give him a hint as to how soon they would arrive back in a human city. So David had stopped asking, knowing they had to arrive in a town at some point.

Gullin gave David a light punch in the shoulder. "Might as well have some fun, if you're tagging along for the ride. You know, some of the girls talk about you. They're hoping you don't have a lass back home."

David didn't reply to that.

"Well, do you?"

"No."

"Now that's a shame. A fellow like you should have a girl. Someone you can show off all that brain of yours to. Ladies like the smart ones."

"I doubt that," David said curtly, but then he made his tone more casual. "I study to better myself, not impress others. Education is a more important matter than frivolous flirting."

"Trust me, you'll learn more from a lady than from any book, boy."

"If you mean learn about love ... books hold all of the best romances in the world—if I were interested in that sort of thing. Writers can imagine unspoiled, true love and not have to think about if that love ever rots after the story finishes. Romantic impulses in real life pale—*would* pale in comparison. But tell me about yourself, Gullin. Do you have a *señora*?"

"Can't say that I do. I was married, once. She passed away a while ago ..." He trailed off, a hardness entering his brow. "She had the 'chat' with you yet?"

"Huh? Who?"

"The mistress. She had the chat with you yet, when you're asleep?" Gullin reiterated.

David raised his eyebrows at him. "Does she appear to all of you in dreams too?"

"She and I used to chat pretty regularly. Been a while now since our last talk." Gullin gave David a stern look. "What'd she tell you?"

David wrinkled a corner of his nose at Gullin's glare. The juggler was awfully touchy when it came to the sphinx. "Nothing much. It wasn't a very long conversation."

Gullin let out a heavy breath. "You just watch what you say to her, you hear? She acts differently 'round you. Don't be doing anything to upset her, got it?"

81

"Fine, fine," David said, putting up his hands in defense. "I'm fine, you're fine, Acacia's fine. Everything's fine."

Gullin suddenly stiffened. "Acacia?"

"Yes, that's the name I've given her. I guess you don't have to call her that, if you don't want to. She seems fine with it."

Gullin opened his mouth to say something, but he came up empty. He looked surprised, then befuddled, and then he just made a faint tense smile and a slight nod. He walked away quickly, leaving David perplexed.

When the gypsies retired to the comfortable lodging within the cave, David stayed outside by the lagoon. He figured that if he was quick, he could give himself a decent enough wash without being seen. But he had not even gotten his shirt off when a voice jumped out from behind him.

"Forgive me for intruding," Nico said as he emerged from the brush. His tone clearly indicated he wasn't sincere about it. "I don't suppose the Lady Sphinx is around? I mean to apologize for my behavior this evening."

David tugged down his shirt, wiping his hands down the front. Before he could reply, Nico rattled on. "By the way, I should address her by her new name. It's only good manners. Tell me, what lovely moniker did you bestow on her?"

"Acacia," David answered suspiciously.

Nico cocked an eyebrow critically, and made a light snort. "Well, one can't account for another's taste. How long have you been with your darling's little rabble?"

"She's not my 'darling.'"

The fox-man chuckled. "That seems unlikely, given the circumstances."

David's expression gave away his confusion.

"For all your supposed genius, you don't know how it works with our kind, do you?" Nico twirled his vest's chain in his fingers. "Have you never wondered why many of the monsters in old tales didn't have names? They were simply called what they were—chimera, hydra, sphinx. A name carries a lot of power with it. For clans of the Drakaina born, it carries so much power, it can determine ownership. Giving one of us a name, a personal one like you humans have, is similar to your tradition of giving ... what is it called? An engagement ring."

The young man's eyes shot wide open. Was the Teumessian joking? "What are you talking about?"

"Come on, don't be stupid. You understand perfectly." Nico scratched himself behind the ear. "I've spent a good deal of time in your world, so I was smart enough to legally name myself. Even have the documents to prove it. It leaves me in complete control, no risk of romantic imprisonment." He made that dirty grin again at David. "But I can only guess it was your idea to give her a name.

You humans don't like things you can't label. I'm sure she didn't oppose it … *not one bit.* I fear perhaps by now she may be in deep sleep, so do give her my apologies, won't you? There's a good boy." He turned and walked away, calling over his shoulder, "I'm sure we'll be seeing a lot more of you now, David. Welcome to the family."

David could only stand there for a long time, alone. He was too stunned to speak.

Acacia had not fallen asleep yet. She had, in fact, become concerned when David did not come into the cave with the others for the night. As she walked out of the cave and around the lagoon, she caught a fleeting glimpse of Nico before he vanished off.

She approached David slowly, gauging him. When he saw her, he stepped away. Then his face grew angry, and his fists clenched.

"Is it really tradition for your kind to take someone who gives you a name, as a mate?" he seethed.

She stopped cold. She could only gaze at him, patiently. Her eyes began to glow.

David thrust an arm over his eyes. "No! Don't try to trick me. I can understand enough of Latin. Just tell me yes or no. Did you allow me to name you, knowing you could claim me for yourself?"

He kept his arm over his eyes as he waited. Then he smelled her sweet, enticing breath in his face. He held his breath, using his free hand to pinch his nose shut. He stepped back, turning around to put his back to her. He knew what she was trying to do. She was trying to calm him down. But he didn't care, there was no amount of sweet breath she could use on him to quell his anger.

"I guess that answers it," he hissed. "Let me tell you something, *Sphinx*, I don't consent to it. You can't keep me, and you can't tell me what to do. I want you to take me back to my world immediately. I have my own life! I have an education, an apprenticeship waiting for me, and a good, secure future. You can't take me away from that. Besides, being a monster's mate is just ... revolting!"

He expected her to react instantly. He expected the mauling, flesh-tearing, and strangling that she undoubtedly wanted to give him. But nothing happened. There was no reaction, not even a sound. David slowly turned to look back at her, keeping one eye shut and the other squinted just in case.

She was gone.

The island was quiet now, a striking contrast to the gala of music and laughter that had permeated the air only a short time ago. Even residents of the magical worlds must sleep eventually, with the exception of the two-headed Amphisbaena, whose front head was resting while the head attached to his tail stayed awake. The attentive head watched David as he walked past through the bounty of ferns and tropical trees and towards the shoreline, before it turned its attention to a wandering mouse scurrying nearby.

David walked down to the beach, which looked out onto the dark sea reflecting the midnight sky. He wondered if it was the same sky that he had always lived beneath, or if maybe the sky was like a mirror and on the other side of it was his world. He gazed out towards the horizon, where he could just make out the cloudy haze of the Curtain. He tested a foot on the water to see if he could still walk across it. His boot dipped into the cool reef, soaking through to his toes. He withdrew his foot and sighed, considering if it would be worth the risk to swim out to sea.

He heard footsteps approaching, and turned to see two of the gypsy women coming towards him. He recognized them; Isabella and a young dancer named Moline. David couldn't imagine that Acacia had sent them in an attempt to retrieve him. Why not just come after him herself? He waited as the women arrived.

"We've come to take you back home," Isabella stated.

David blinked in surprise. "She sent you to do this?"

"Yes," replied Moline. "She spoke to us in our sleep. She said you do not belong with us, and that we can guide you back to your home through the Curtain."

"But how? Can we do that without her? How do we even get over to it?"

"She taught us how. Come." Isabella held her hand out to David, and Moline did the same. A sense of relief washed over David as he took the women by their hands. The three of them stepped out onto the water, and easily remained above the surface. With each step, the Curtain got rapidly closer, almost lurching forwards towards them, and David clung tighter to his guides' hands. He kept repeating to himself, *Almost home, almost home … then I can wake up and all this will have been a silly dream …*

Atop a cliff overlooking the ocean, not far from the nests where the sirens slept soundly, the sphinx was sitting quietly, holding her paw over her face to mask her tears. She did not quite understand herself, why she let this boy hurt her so. Was it any surprise, the way he reacted? He did not understand her culture, and he felt betrayed. But he had named her. She knew from the moment he had intruded on her camp that he was unlike the others. But he was human too; why should he have been so different as to not find her … revolting …

She felt a tap on her shoulder. She looked up to see a silk handkerchief dangling in front of her nose.

"Wipe your nose. You look unbecoming, your face all puffed and red like that," her orange-haired cousin remarked.

Acacia snarled at him, hissing for him to go away.

Nico shrugged and tucked his handkerchief in

his pocket. "Sulking in self-loathing, Cousin? I don't blame you. You are difficult to deal with. But, if it's any consolation, it's no real loss. Humans are overly abundant. If you fancy that breed, you have more than an ample selection to replace that one."

The sphinx sprang up at him, snagging Nico by the collar of his suit with her claws. She snapped her teeth at him, grazing his nose.

The Teumessian grinned. "Temper, temper, Cousin … I'm sorry, *Acacia*. Enjoy your name, because it's all you're going to have left."

She narrowed her eyes, tilting her head.

"You see, I wanted to make sure you were distracted long enough for my friends to get your 'favorite' lost in the Curtain, past the point where you could do anything to stop them."

The sphinx's eyes widened in panic. She knew her cousin was not lying. She took off like a bolt of lightning from the cliff, spreading her black wings and catching the wind. She flew as fast as possible, creating such a powerful gust with her wing-beats that it awakened the sirens from sleep, believing a hurricane was approaching.

Nico watched his cousin speed off, knowing she would be too late.

The Curtain rolled about like an infuriated storm cloud, but the two gypsies led David forward into it without hesitation. The young man held his breath as the Curtain wrapped around him, and he was pulled forward into its opaque haze. He gripped the hands that guided him, unable to even see the two women by his side.

And then they weren't by his side.

He was alone.

"Isabella? Moline??" David felt a shock of fear ripple through him as he reached out, trying to find the women. "Where are you? I can't see anything!"

Then he heard giggling. Not the type of giggling that two human women would make, but a whimsical, child-like giggling he had heard only earlier that evening. For a second, he saw the silhouettes of two petite shapes in the fog, and then they leaped away like antelope, light and bouncy in a way only nymphs could move.

The Teumessian's nymphs! They had tricked him!

David took one step in an attempt to get out of the fog, but instantly he was pitched downwards, tumbling head over heels. He saw himself sinking down beneath the water, away from the cloud of the Curtain and deep into shadow, but there was no sound, no feeling, no sense of drowning or cold. It was nothingness, just a draining of color and light until disorientation set in, and David was not sure how long he had been falling before he became unconscious.

CHAPTER FIVE

David awoke to the sound of someone screeching at him, in a dialect he had never heard before.

He struggled to awaken. His head was sore and his bones ached. He could feel that he was moving, and that he was lying on something scaly and wet. Opening his eyes, he saw a river surrounding him, and grassy shores swiftly rushing past him. Looking down, he found that he was lying on something large, splotched with white, orange and brown. Two massive fins paddled on each side, and a long tail swiveled to and fro behind.

He was on a koi fish the size of a boat.

If that was not strange enough, there was an unusual animal dangling by its sinewy arm from a tree branch that stretched out over the river. It was roughly the size of a cat, having the body of a tortoise, the head and limbs of a monkey, and it was green all over. It was shrieking at David, in what he could tell were words, but none of any language he'd ever studied.

The fish slowed down to a halt beneath the turtle-monkey. The monkey piped a few quick words at David.

The young man sat up on the fish's back, blinking wearily at the chirping peculiarity.

"I don't understand what you're saying," David called up to the turtle-monkey. A few days ago, he would have found talking to a monkey ridiculous. A lot had changed since then.

The green monkey jumped down from its branch, landing squarely on David's chest. David gasped. The monkey tipped his head forward, and David could see three holes in the top of it. Out of these holes poured a liquid, which splashed directly into David's mouth. He choked on the liquid, but could not keep from swallowing it.

"What was that for?" he spat.

His anger dissipated instantly when the turtle-monkey, in clear, comprehensible words, replied, "That was so you could understand what I'm saying, Bald Butt!"

David's jaw dropped so wide, crows could have flown into it.

"You're not from around here, are you?" The monkey pulled and poked at David's clothing. "You're lucky Kami here found you, or you'd be a drowned sack of bones. Where'd you come from?"

"I was ... walking through the Curtain ..."

"The Curtain! Now humans are walking through the Curtain. There goes the neighborhood." The turtle-monkey sat down across from David upon the fish's back, and the fish resumed swimming. "Lost, are you?"

"Yes … where am I, exactly?"

"The Kyoto province."

David furrowed his eyebrows. "Uh …"

"The rest should be obvious. You're speaking Japanese right now."

Japan? How had he ended up in Japan? David knew where Japan was from his world maps at home, although his knowledge of the land was limited. All he knew was that it was halfway around the world from where he wanted to be! "How did I get here? I was in France when we went through the Curtain the first time …"

The monkey scratched his chin. "France …never heard of it. The Curtain is tricky. You can walk into it in one place, and when you walk out, you're someplace else. I don't travel through it much myself. Got everything I need here."

David sighed, resting his arms on his knees. "I don't suppose you could help me get back through the Curtain?"

"Nope. Not unless …" The turtle-monkey had an eager shine in his eyes. "Do you have any cucumbers?"

David shook his head. "Can't say that I do."

"That's a shame. Can I have some of your blood?"

"My blood? No!"

"Drat. No one ever says yes."

"Are you … a vampire?"

The monkey rubbed his head. "If a vampire likes

cucumbers and blood, then yes! But around here, they call me a kappa." He rapped his fingers on the belly of his tortoise shell body. "And I'd much rather have a cucumber than blood. Nice and crunchy." He grinned, showing his pointy fangs.

David took a moment to think. He didn't have any money on him to arrange a means of travel to get back home. He pondered if he could secretly hitch a ride on a steam train, the way he heard vagabonds did, but even if locomotives ran in this area, it wouldn't do much good since Japan was an island. He had no idea where to find a port in this place, and he doubted this giant fish he was riding would be willing to swim him all the way home.

"Could you please help me get back into the Curtain? I have no other way to get home," David pleaded.

The kappa stuck his tongue out at him. "Why should I? You don't have any cucumbers."

"I can get you cucumbers, if that's what you want! I need to find the sphinx. She'll know how to get me back home."

"Sphinx?" The kappa's face lighted up. "Does a sphinx have cucumbers?"

David grunted in frustration. "Stop thinking about cucumbers for a minute! I need to get home. The Curtain is the only way. I would be eternally grateful if you would help me, or direct me to someone who can."

The kappa scratched his head. "I think I know someone who could help. He's the smartest creature I know. And he always has something good to eat."

"*Gracias!* Will you take me to him?"

"Uh uh uh." The turtle-monkey shook his head, but he did so carefully so not to spill the water in his head holes. "I can't go too far from water. My head will dry out. And my friend lives way out across the fields, and there are big men with swords that dwell there. Nope, can't go."

David felt apprehensive about the armed men, but surely now that he could speak Japanese, he could reason with them. He thought for a moment, and then said, "Would you take me if I … let you have a little— just a little—blood?" He held out his wrist with great reluctance.

The kappa licked his lips at the exposed wrist, but then gave David a doubtful glare. "You're not a bad blood, are you? Rotten, sick blood? Humans only give rotten, sick stuff away that they don't want."

"No, it's good, as far as I know."

The kappa took David's hand, and gave him a sharp nip on the finger with one of its fangs. He tested one drop of blood, smacking his lips. "Not bad. But it would be better with sake. My friend has some. I'll take you to him, very quickly, and then I'll take your payment with sake. Maybe he has cucumbers today, too." The kappa's face bloomed with bliss at the thought.

The countryside of Kyoto was breathtaking. The fields of long grass swayed rhythmically in the wind, and in the distance, mountains watched over the land like patient monks in meditation. Everything was alien to David, but at the same time it had a familiar tranquility that reminded him of home. As they walked, the kappa led David as quickly as he could, either because of the enigmatic men with swords that were supposedly nearby, or because the liquid in the holes in his head was rapidly drying up.

"Who are these men you mentioned before?" David asked. "The ones who have weapons? Are they bandits?"

The kappa kept his voice low, although there was no sign of anyone being around. "They used to be honorable warriors who were dedicated to serving their masters. But now they have no masters. So they don't know what to do. Sometimes they become bandits, sometimes hired soldiers for war. But the men in this place … they are not nice men. They prey on villagers and wayward travelers for money. And they don't much care for foreigners either. If we run into them, you're a dead duck."

David made a soft gulp. Maybe he should have stayed on the fish.

They made their way into the lush greenery of a forest. The kappa hopped from tree trunk to tree trunk as David made his way through the brush. He tried to enjoy the quiet bliss of the forest, but his active imagination planted hidden warriors behind each tree, ready to impale him with bow and arrow and sword. He brushed off the flies that were congregating on his neck and arms, drawn in by his drenching sweat. David was thankful that the canopy was thick enough to shade him from the glaring sun, but after walking for what must have been over an hour, the heat and exhaustion were flaying him mercilessly.

They came upon a dirt road running through the forest, a path having been trampled by many horse hooves. The kappa sniffed at the dirt road, and the air.

"Good, we are almost there," he said. But then he snapped his head down the road behind them, and his ears twitched. His eyes grew wide, and he scrambled up the nearest tree in a blur of green.

"Hey, where are you going?" David demanded, but then he heard what the kappa had heard: approaching hoofbeats. He looked back to see two figures on horseback riding his way at a fast pace, and he knew they had already spotted him. He wasn't sure whether to run or stand his ground—maybe these weren't bandits, but the local patrol of a nearby village and he could explain himself. But being a foreigner may not work in his interest, so he dashed off the road and ran as fast as his feet could carry him, darting between the trees.

The men on their chestnut brown horses followed in pursuit, artfully steering their steeds around the tall tree trunks. David heard the sharp thwack of something behind him hitting a tree, and the whooshing sound of something fast flying past his head.

They're shooting at me!

The ground suddenly sloped down drastically, and at the pace David was running he couldn't adjust fast enough to keep from stumbling. He tumbled down the hill like a rolling barrel, thankfully avoiding any trees and rocks, but when he reached the bottom he fell straight into a muddy ditch. By the time he climbed up and out, the two horsemen had arrived and were aiming arrows at his head.

David's heart beat rapidly as he thought of what to do. He put his hands up, saying, "I don't have anything you want. I'm a stranger here, and I have no money or possessions. Just let me be on my way."

One of the horsemen, a ronin displaying deep scars on his face, curled his lip. "You are trespassing on our land. Anyone who travels through here must pay us tribute. If you have no money, we will take those fine clothes you are wearing."

Being naked was better than being dead, but then what would keep these men from killing him after he handed over his clothes? The only reason they probably weren't killing him now was because they didn't want blood all over his apparel, whether they were planning on selling the material or keeping it for themselves. David tried a bluff. "Look, I can get you money. My friend has a gold stash out here in these woods that I was coming to get for him. I'll let you have it if you don't kill me."

The two ronin glanced at each other, and the one who had not spoken yet gave a quick nod. They kept their arrows locked on David. "Show us," the first man said.

David walked along, while the two men followed him. His mind was going at rapid-fire pace to think of how he was going to get out of this one. His bluff was buying him time, but it wouldn't last for long. Where was that bloody kappa anyway? He could be of help right now.

After a long walk, the two ronin growing more impatient with each step, they came to a wooden bridge crossing a river. David paused as a quickly-crafted plan came to his mind.

"It's tucked away in a dirt mound under the bridge," he told the two ronin. "I'll go get it."

"No," one of the ronin barked. "You will stay here. He will go get it," he confirmed, beckoning his friend to go look.

David's heart sank. He was hoping to slip under the bridge and swim away downstream. He was a good swimmer and hopefully he'd dodge any arrows the ronin might fire after him. But it was clear that the two ronin had already suspected that sort of escape attempt. One ronin dismounted his horse and made his way down the river bank. The second ronin continued to keep his eye on David, arrow at the ready.

David held his breath as he waited for the man to come back, furious that there was nothing there, and beat him to death.

A loud skull-shattering crack broke the silence.

The ronin next to David toppled off his horse, unconscious. A large shape galloped past David, and he could see it was a third man on horseback, only this man was draped head to toe in white and riding a horse with a docked tail cut short to three inches. The second ronin scurried back up from the bridge to try and get the bow he had left in his horse's saddle, but before he could, the mystery rider charged him, his horse rearing up wildly. The ronin staggered backwards to keep from getting kicked by the horse's hooves, and he fell down into the river. The rushing water swept him away a good distance before he made his way back to shore. David and the white-clad horseman watched as the ronin took flight into the woods.

David released his breath in a long exhale. He turned to thank his rescuer, but then hesitated. Could this be a rival bandit taking out the competition? For all he knew, this horseman could be even deadlier than the two men who had accosted him.

The horseman casually rode over to David. His face was masked by a white balaclava, so all that was visible were his eyes, which David noticed were solid black. He pointed to the horse of the unconscious ronin, gesturing for David to get on it. A practiced rider, David jumped up onto the horse's back and beckoned it to follow his rescuer.

"Why did you help me?" David asked as they plodded along.

The man did not answer. David then noticed something else. The man's horse did not have a docked tail. It was not even a horse's tail. It was a small brownish tuft of fur.

"Since I saved you," the mystery man said, "I think it's only fair that you give me a ride."

"But, you already have a ..."

Before David could finish, the man and horse both shrank and changed shape. In their place was a small striped badger. The badger sauntered over, balancing on his hind legs.

"Well?" the badger huffed. "Are you going to give me a ride or not?"

CHAPTER SIX

"That was fun!" the badger laughed as he balanced on his hind legs atop David's head. "I haven't had a good tussle like that since I beat that smelly Oni at arm-wrestling."

The badger had directed David through the forest to a small shack surrounded by a modest garden. Within the hut, there was not much: woven mats on the floor, a brown kotatsu-style dining table and cushions, a fire pit, and a horde of empty bottles. The kappa was already there when they arrived, trying to pull his finger out of a bottle in which he was now stuck.

"Ah, you are all right?" the kappa said as David stepped into the hut.

"No thanks to you," David replied sourly. "You ran off when I needed your help."

The kappa frowned. "Do not be sore at me. When those two men chased after you, I came straight here to get Tanuki to help. He is good at tricking thieves."

The badger Tanuki smiled broadly as he jumped down from David's head. "I am good at many things. It's nice to be the most divine creature in all of Kyoto. But

Brother Kappa, aren't you worried of your head drying out, this far from the river?"

"I hoped you had a little sake left, to keep my head wet." The kappa, exasperated that he could not free himself from the bottle's hold, began banging his glass finger prison on the floor.

Tanuki shook his head with a smirk. In one quick spin, he transformed himself into a large green bottle. He floated off the floor and hung in the air over the kappa, where he tipped over and splashed sake over the turtle-monkey until he was drenched from head to tail. Tanuki resumed his normal shape, grasped the neck of the bottle that held the kappa, and popped off the bottle with a firm pull.

"There, your finger is free," Tanuki said triumphantly.

The kappa licked absentmindedly at the sake soaking his fur.

David cleared his throat. "Tanuki, is it? I was hoping you could help me. I need to get back through the Curtain, and the kappa said you would know how."

Tanuki twitched his nose. "The Curtain? I don't like going through the Curtain. Too foggy. I get lost a lot."

"But the kappa said—"

"I said Tanuki is the most clever friend I know," the kappa corrected him, and he shook his shell to allow some of the sake that had seeped down into it to escape. "I never said he would actually take you through the Curtain."

David gritted his teeth. "Then you brought me all this way for nothing??"

A strange voice filled the air. "What is all this noise?"

Instantly, the kappa and Tanuki froze and were silent. A lean, tall figure emerged from behind a sliding, paper-screen door at the back of the hut. He was an ancient man, with a long white beard that almost dragged the floor. He had a short top-knot on his otherwise bald head, and a long blue robe hung on his frail body. The sage's fingernails were long but clean, and he used them to stroke his cascading beard. The smells of the sea flowed from all around him. He had a length of black cloth wrapped over his eyes, and David could make out the lines of deep scars peeking out from the bandage.

"Who is this stranger you have brought to my home?" the blind man asked.

David bowed in respect to the elder, and he took a deep breath before answering. "I am David Sandoval. I come from a place far away from here. I was hoping someone could help me get back home."

"Hmm." The sage moved smoothly through the room as if not blind at all, and he sat down on one of the cushions at the table. Tanuki went to the fire pit where a tea kettle was boiling on the fire. The kappa fetched a teacup from the other side of the room and set it down in front of the sage. Tanuki poured him tea, and then both kappa and badger took seats at the table next to the old man.

He must be their master, David thought.

The man gestured for David to take the remaining seat at the table, which he did.

"You wish to travel through the Curtain to get home?" the old man inquired.

David nodded. "Yes, that was how I got here in the first place. It's a long story, but if I can get back into the Curtain, then I can find Aca—the sphinx. She'll know how to send me back."

"The sphinx." The man stroked his beard again. "Ah, yes, the handsome young lady from the deserts of the far West. How is she these days?"

David was not sure how to answer at first. Did this old man really know Acacia? Was he from across the Curtain too? "I haven't known her that long."

The sage nodded, and sipped from his teacup. "I'm afraid going back into the Curtain is not that simple. As you have discovered, you can enter the Curtain in one place of our world, and end up in someplace else you never intended. Only those who know how to navigate the hidden corridors of the Curtain can go where they wish."

"Do you know how to travel through it, Mister …?"

"Mister?" The badger was positively mortified. "You do not call the master plain old 'mister'!"

The old man raised a hand to Tanuki to silence him. "My name is Yofune Nushi. And yes, I am familiar with the Curtain."

"That's great! Then you can help lead me back home." David caught himself, and added, "I mean, if you would, Master Yofune." He was embarrassed, since he did not know if Yofune's blindness would be a hindrance in the Curtain.

"Is that where your path is meant to lead you, Sandoval-san?"

David lapsed into momentary silence, struggling to understand why Yofune would ask him such a question. "I do have a path. I am to be an apprentice to a very good teacher in Paris. I am to finish my studies and make my way in the world. I had my life perfectly planned until that … that thieving sphinx took me away!"

Yofune's face tightened into a frown. "Why would the sphinx take you away?"

"I don't know!" David's eyes wandered away from the sage. "Well … I did invade her camp and tried to … stab her … but honestly, who kidnaps someone who tries to kill them? Why not just kill me and have it done with?"

"Indeed, why not?"

The question struck David with a thought that he hadn't contemplated before. Why hadn't Acacia killed him that night? Gullin said the men themselves would have gladly beaten him to death if Acacia had wished it. He had assumed that she had wanted to possess him like a pet, as retaliation for his audacity to even think he could slay her. It was the "keep your friends close, and your enemies closer" line of thinking. But she hadn't mistreated him or abused her power over him. If anything, she had been constantly stung by his rejection and repellence of her, and she had refrained from hurting him. Why had she gone to such lengths to try and keep winning his trust, when ripping his throat out would have been a more predictable action for a …

"Maybe she wants to prove she's not a monster," David thought aloud.

"What defines monstrosity?" Yofune folded his hands into the folds of his sleeves. "Is it having a form that is not acceptable? Is it how sharp your teeth are, or if you have claws instead of fingernails? Or does it reside, in some invisible shape, inside all of us, Sandoval-san?"

David was silent.

"There is an invisible shape inside of her," Yofune continued. "But it is not what makes her a monster. It is what makes her a prisoner, much more than she ever made you. She has lost the ability to speak, has she not?"

"Not entirely … but she told me, in a dream, that talking aloud risks her health. When she tries to speak, she only speaks in Latin, and it hurts her inside." David sensed Yofune already knew his curiosity as to what was causing Acacia's condition.

The old man nodded solemnly. "Latin is one of the purest of languages, and the one her clan would have spoken since their first beginnings. It has magical properties, the root of charms and spells, thus it does provide some protection for her, and does not wound her as greatly as speaking a modern language. But even then, it cannot stop the shape from devouring each syllable she utters, and thus is slowly devouring her from the inside out."

"What is this 'shape' you keep mentioning?"

Tanuki got a worried look on his face, and began shivering. The kappa looked confused, scratching his drying scalp. Yofune poured a little tea into the monkey's head holes. The kappa yelped, stung by the heat of the tea.

"Does this shape look like a cucumber?" the kappa wondered. "I could really use a cucumber right about now ..."

"This has nothing to do with the cravings of your stomach," Yofune replied firmly.

Tanuki put his paws to his head, squeezing his eyes shut. "Do not speak of stomachs! Not when you have mentioned that horrid Shade! Oh, dear, dear grandfather Raiju! Poor Raiju!" The badger squirmed, swerving his head from side to side. He shifted his shape into a small cloud that swirled around the room, weeping big blobs of raindrops. The kappa got up and walked around beneath him to keep his head holes filled with water.

"I'm afraid our friend Tanuki knows too well about the Shades of Nyx," Yofune sighed.

"The Shades of Nyx?" David felt like he had read that name somewhere before in one of his mythological texts. Nyx ...

Tanuki resumed his badger shape after he had dried himself of tears. "A Shade of Nyx was put inside the belly of my grandfather Raiju. He was the spirit of lightning, a shapeshifter who favored the shape of the badger. He was well known for his swiftness as he jumped from tree to tree in a flourish of white fire. But then … he was consumed by a yellow Shade, and it ripped him open and took his beloved gift back to Nyx!"

"It was a Shade designed to steal from Raiju his speed," Yofune explained.

David tried to piece all of this information together. "What, exactly, are these shades? What are they meant to do? And who is Nyx?"

Yofune arose from the table, and went to stand by the fire pit. "Nyx is a goddess of night. She is daughter of Chaos, and mother to many. She birthed Sleep, Fate, Age, Strife, and even Death. Her power is unfathomable, and even the mightiest of gods fear her."

The kappa gulped loudly. David refrained from doing the same, although his unease was just as strong.

Yofune continued. "Madam Nyx controls the spectrum of both light and shadow of the moon and stars. Her shades are various colors she has woven from her spectrum, and they act as an extension of her will. She finds ways to implant them into those whom she envies, whose abilities she covets."

"You mean, she envied Raiju for his speed, and

that's why she put a Shade in him? To have his speed for herself?" David asked.

"I don't believe it is for herself," the old man replied. "But she desires to collect the most prized traits from magical creatures, each that embody the best of a natural talent or skill. I have heard that she used brown Shades to take the strength of titans, and blue Shades to steal the songs from muses. Your sphinx, I believe, has been stricken with a shade in order to be stripped of her infamous cunning."

David folded his hands together. He stared down at the tabletop, rather surprised that he was feeling badly for the sphinx. "Could ... this Shade of Nyx ... will it kill Acacia?"

Yofune smirked. "An odd concern for a man who admitted he intended to do something similar. But I believe you just referred to your sphinx by a familiar name?'

David clamped his mouth shut. Did Yofune also know about the sphinx's matrimonial tradition?

"Ah." Yofune pulled a small sprig of some exotic plant from his robe and crumpled it between his fingers. He sprinkled it onto the fire pit, which caused the flames to crackle and flicker a bright scarlet. "No doubt she is already looking for you. A sphinx is very devoted when she believes she has found her life partner. Come here."

The young man paused, but he stood up slowly and

walked over to the sage. The words "life partner" stabbed his brain like knitting needles.

"Sit." Yofune motioned for David to sit down next to him on the floor. "You said the sphinx talked to you in a dream. I am opening a dream path through this fire. You need to relax and concentrate on the flames. It will put you in a half-sleep, and if she is searching for you, she will sense you in that state. Then you may tell her where you are, and she can come for you."

"Didn't you say you know how to travel through the Curtain? Couldn't you guide me back home?"

Yofune sighed with a long, tired exhale. "Is that the choice you truly wish to make? To go back to your life of ignorant bliss, knowing what you know now?" The old man turned to David, and even through his bandages David could feel Yofune's burning gaze. "Do you not think you were made aware of the world beyond the Curtain for a purpose?"

David wrinkled his brow. "Why did you want me to know all of this? These 'Shades,' this Madam Nyx, is beyond my control, don't you think?"

"Do *you* think?"

"Of course I think …" He stopped. The hanging silence brought David around to a realization that sent electric shocks through his gut. "Are you saying this was meant to happen? Did Acacia actually choose me to do something about all of this?"

"That is something only she knows. All I can tell you

is this: any traveler who has found his way to me, was meant to find me. Those travelers who live after they find me, were clearly destined for a grander purpose."

David blanched. "Who ... live?"

Yofune smiled. "You are still here. That is good. Now look into the fire."

David almost declined, worried about what could happen while he was hypnotized by the fire. But he found that a part of him did want to find Acacia, to make sure she and her gypsy family were all right. He was even concerned for Gullin, as gruff and odd as he was. David gazed into the dancing flames, the colors rippling up and billowing out as if breathing, flowing, pulsating with the rhythm of the earth. Soon that same rhythm found its way into his mind, a quiet drumming that beckoned him to march forward. While his body remained seated on the floor inside the hut, another part of him journeyed into the scarlet fire. Suddenly he was exposed to a whole universe of secret pathways, and he was rapidly traversing down one after another as quickly as a soul can fly.

CHAPTER SEVEN

Navigating the dream paths was exhausting, even as an astral projection.

David did not have much control over where he was going, but the farther he went, the more he realized how various dream paths crossed one another. At first, he thought the images he was seeing were figments of his imagination, since they did not have precise shape or detail. His sight eventually adjusted, however, and he could see that he was surrounded by thousands of people, creatures, and manifested emotions. Most did not acknowledge him, for they were involved in matters of their own, but a few faces watched him as he passed by, as if he were some fleeting whimsy.

Then he noticed several of these fellow path-walkers were more pronounced in shape than others, and their eyes held a sharp, penetrating gaze much like that he had felt when Acacia had spoken to him in his dream. They, too, observed him as he went by, but he could tell that they must be like the sphinx, in that they had the talent to choose how they wanted to appear in others' dreams, and how to construct the environments of dreams.

How was he going to find Acacia in all of this? It was not even for certain she would know he was here, and he did not know if her ability to enter his dreams worked if she did not know he was asleep. He considered calling out for her, but found he was without a voice.

How long am I supposed to wander around here? he thought. *I'm never going to find that sphinx in all this!*

May I assist you?

The sudden voice caught David by surprise. He couldn't see where it had come from, and it was impossible to know who had spoken to him among the multitude of dream shapes. He tried to keep strict control over his thoughts. *Are you talking to me?*

Naturally.

Who are you? David asked.

My name is Hypnos. My sons and I are the keepers of this realm. I take care of all humans as they sleep. But I can tell you are not sleeping. You have had a dream path open to you. What are you searching for?

David wondered if this unseen entity was trustworthy.

I promise you, I intend you no harm, came a calm reply.

Where are you? Can I at least see you?

I am all around you. I am Sleep itself. But, if you would prefer, I will take a shape for you.

Instantly, the image of a man appeared. It was hard to describe what Hypnos looked like, other than there were two dark blue wings that sprouted from his head, just above his ears. He seemed to be ever shifting his features, but at the same time his image was constant. All that could be said was he was handsome—probably handsome to everyone, no matter what their tastes.

David remembered that Yofune had mentioned that Sleep was one of the sons of Nyx. Sensing David's thought, Hypnos nodded in affirmation.

Now, did you say you were looking for the sphinx? Hypnos inquired.

Yes, David answered.

That at least narrows it down. Wait a moment.

Hypnos vanished back into the dream atmosphere. He caused a ripple effect that echoed David's thoughts, and David could hear it reverberating throughout the dream pathways. It was dizzying, and David wondered if Hypnos was playing a game with him. But after a moment, something echoed back towards him, bouncing from one dream creature to the next as if they were all playing catch with a rubber ball.

David, is that you? Where are you?

It was her voice!

Impulsively, he thought his answer back. *I'm on a dream path. I'm surrounded by thousands of people, and I feel like I can't stop moving.*

The same ripple sent out his thought, and he received her response immediately. *Think of the place we were in your dream the night we first talked. Keep concentrating on it so you can send the vision back to me. I'll meet you there.*

Hypnos' voice returned. *I will leave you two be, for now. But, David, I know you have more questions for me. Ask when you are ready.*

David wanted to tell him he was ready to ask now, about Nyx, her Shades, and if Hypnos knew what the Shade would do to Acacia. Before he could, however, he found himself in a blank white space, like an unpainted empty room. He figured Hypnos had put him here to meet Acacia, so David concentrated on recreating the same dreamscape as before, a grassy shore overlooking the shimmering sea, and a small birch tree and gently flowing winds.

Almost as soon as he was done completing his dreamscape, the beautiful woman he had met there before appeared. For a moment, Acacia stared at him with her green, gold-rimmed eyes. David felt a creeping dread about what she might say or do. She couldn't be happy with him, after the way he had spoken to her.

She raced to him and grabbed him in a tight, unyielding embrace.

I am so glad you are all right, she projected into his mind. There was a gentle joy in her tone.

"You're not mad at me?" he asked.

It was not your fault. Nico tricked you into getting lost in the Curtain. He is an awful, wicked brute.

"But what I said before, at the lagoon … I know I hurt you. I'm sorry."

It's all right. You felt deceived. I could not explain to

you at the time, about what Nico told you. She released him from the hug, and looked into his eyes. *Yes, it is true, in my family line, bequeathing a familiar name means establishing a bond much like those of mates. But it is not binding. I would not hold you to it if you did not wish it.*

A wave of relief washed over David. He did catch, however, the disappointed tone in Acacia's voice. "Are you still at the sirens' island?" he asked.

I have been searching everywhere on both sides of the Curtain for you. Where are you? Are you someplace safe?

"I'm in Japan. I'm staying with a man named Yofune Nushi, who says he knows you. Do you know where he lives?"

Acacia's body tensed up, and concern was reflected in her gaze. *Yofune Nushi? Has he treated you well? He has not hurt you, has he?*

"He said given that I am still alive, that's a good thing."

Acacia smiled and nodded, and she rested her head on David's shoulder. *I know we don't have much time, as I must bring you back and make sure my family is all right. I left them in the care of my sisters. They will guard them until our return. But, for this brief moment, I can be at peace again.*

He had to admit, it was a rather nice moment.

The inevitable question about Acacia's affliction crossed his mind, and he waited silently to see if she would read his thoughts and respond. She did not, however, which caused him to wonder if she really did not know what he wanted to ask, or if she knew and was refusing to comment. She looked so content and lost in the moment they were sharing, maybe she was not even attempting to access his mind.

He knew that now was the time to ask, while she could speak to him without the Shade harming her. "Acacia, Yofune told me that you have something inside of you that is hurting you whenever you speak. He called it a Shade of Nyx."

Acacia held him closer. *None of that now,* she said calmly. *No questions.*

"But Yofune said this Shade is deadly—"

I won't discuss it.

"I want to. Is there something that can be done to get that Shade out of you—"

She broke the embrace and held him away from her, glowering at him. *If there was something that could be done, I'd have done it a long time ago. There is no point in speaking about something you cannot change. Do not bring it up again.*

When David remained silent, she took it as a consensus to her request. She held him close again, shutting her eyes.

"I just want to help you," he told her.

She sighed, and rested her head against his shoulder. *I appreciate that. What you can do for me is not concern yourself with it. From the moment you found me, I have found a peace with you that I have found with no other living being. I wish to keep it that way. Do not trouble me by being troubled yourself.*

David smirked. "You found peace with me, when I came looking to slay you?"

They say you find what you're looking for where you least expect it.

"What were you looking for?"

Acacia abruptly jerked her head up. *Something is not right ... Gullin ...*

The landscape melted away, as if an artist had splashed paint thinner over a fresh masterpiece. Then Acacia was racing through the world of Sleep with such ferocity that David was sure that if he had been in his body, his flesh would have peeled straight off his bones from the sheer speed of their flight. The rosy haze of the sleep world faded to purple to indigo to black. The only reason David knew when they had come to a halt was because there was a discernable shape in front of them.

The shape was Gullin, or a muted version of him, a reflection seen through a powdered mirror. At first he did not seem to see them. He was staring at nothing, with no expression, much like one of the Jenglots when deprived of blood-warmth. Acacia reached out towards Gullin, touching him on the cheek, and she cooed a soft melody, not in as lovely a voice as her siren sisters, but pleasant and silken.

Gullin became more saturated in color, and his form solidified. His consciousness awakened, and he saw the sphinx before him. His face was like that of a son's who had been reunited with a long lost mother.

"Mistress, you found us!" He realized her form was not the usual, and he looked around at the blackness in which they were suspended. "This is a dream, isn't it? But it is you, the real you." He glanced at David beside her, and tried to cover his grimace with a smile. "And you, too. Glad you're alive, boyo."

Gullin, what is wrong? Acacia asked. *You were not sleeping, for you were trapped in this dark space unwillingly. You were unconscious.*

"Cast that bloody dog down to the pit!" Gullin growled. "That devil with a fox tail claimed that since you ran off after … *him* …" David could tell that he had meant to call him something else, but chose not to in front of Acacia, "that you had abandoned the rest of us and so we were free property for the taking. The sirens weren't going to let him get his paws on us, but then one of his 'friends' came at his call, and tore up the island until he drove everyone off. I tried to fight 'im off …" He looked away in shame. "That fiend was just too big, too strong … knocked me clean out …"

The sphinx's eyes flared with a gold and green fire. *My cousin will pay for this*, she said with dark, brewing malice. She turned back to David, holding his hands. *I must go and protect my family. I will come for you once they are safe. Stay where you are, and let Yofune know I will come as soon as I can. Let him know, if he tries to harm one hair on your head, I will do worse than that young maiden did to his eyes.*

David nodded, knowing he had to let Acacia go for now. She and Gullin vanished from his sight. He felt himself yanked backwards, and he had the sensation of being a drowning man pulled from the water.

He was staring at the fire pit, back in his own body. He stood up, staggering from wooziness, and started towards the door.

"Where are you going?" Yofune asked.

"I have to go help the others," David replied. "The Teumessian took Acacia's family. He has a monster holding them prisoner. I have to go help them."

"Go and fight a monster?" The kappa ducked his head down into his shell. "Why would you want to do that?"

"A good question," Yofune agreed. "I thought you had no admiration for the sphinx. You said you wished to find her so she could take you home."

David ran his fingers through his hair in frustration. "Yes, I know, and she said she would come back for me, but—"

"Ah, I get it," Tanuki said. "He wants to make sure the monster doesn't eat her before she can take him home."

"No, that's not it!" David snapped.

120

Yofune took a step towards David. "Then why do you wish to help her?"

"Because it's my fault they're in trouble! Nico is doing all of this because I embarrassed him in front of everyone. He's mad at me, and Acacia ..." He rubbed his aching temples. "None of this would have happened if I hadn't gotten involved. And whatever monster this is that Nico has holding them, and Acacia's health being so bad, it could ..."

"You care about her."

David took a deep breath. He gave a quick nod.

Yofune stroked his beard. "Do you possess any item that belongs to her? Something with her scent?"

David rummaged through his pockets, realizing that he didn't have much except for his handmade cross and that pouch of pellets that Gullin had given him. The pouch would have to do. If it still had Gullin's scent, it would lead him to Acacia as well. He extracted the pouch and handed it to Tanuki.

Tanuki took the pouch over to Yofune, who took a quick sniff of it and snorted. "These herbs make it difficult to detect your friend's scent." He took another sniff of it. "Fortunately, your friend is incredibly potent. This will do."

Tanuki returned the pouch to David, who pocketed it. "If I may ask, how is this going to help us find Acacia's family?"

Yofune did not answer him. "Tanuki, I will need

you to be my eyes. It has been a long time since I have ventured from this forest. I will need guidance."

Tanuki nodded with excited enthusiasm. "Yes, Master Yofune!"

David fumbled for words. "Master Yofune, no offense, but I don't feel right putting a blind elder of your ... wisdom ... in danger—"

Before he could finish, Yofune's robes rapidly grew in length and breadth, the cloth shifting into plates of thick, glossy scales as blue as the sea. The blind man's body stretched and coiled around in serpentine slenderness, filling the room. His face elongated into a long muzzle, and his underside was covered in ice-white bristles from his chin to the tip of his newly formed tail. Two short antlers sprouted from his head, and his arms and legs twisted around into stubby but muscular crocodilian appendages. The black bandages fell from his eyes, since his head was now five times larger, and it was clear that Yofune's eyes had been scratched out by a knife. In less than four seconds, the sage had been replaced by a sea dragon, a leviathan as ancient as the earth and ocean.

Tanuki jumped atop Yofune's head, positioning himself like a captain at the helm of a ship.

"I will determine if my blindness or 'wisdom' is a problem," Yofune Nushi retorted in a voice that would make thunder fall silent in fear. "And, Sandoval-san, you may stop the flattery. I'm *old*."

David, stunned by the sudden dragon before him, weakly nodded. "Yessir."

"Now get on my back, and be quick about it." Yofune curled around, exposing a spot right above his shoulder blades. David hesitated at first, but then quickly climbed on so as not to anger Yofune by making him wait. He barely sat down before Yofune took off like a gale wind, bursting from the hut and splintering the doorframe as he went.

The kappa, left behind, ambled outside and around to the back of the hut, watching Yofune and his passengers disappear into the forest. "What am I supposed to do??" the kappa called.

He spotted the ripe cucumbers growing in the garden. The broadest smile crossed his face.

"I'll stay on guard here until you get back," he shouted. He picked up a nice fat cucumber and hugged it like a lost friend. "Don't you worry, your friend Kappa isn't going to leave you all alone …"

CHAPTER EIGHT

The countryside of Kyoto whooshed beneath them as Yofune Nushi flew just above the trees, low enough that David feared that they might be spotted. But neither Yofune nor Tanuki seemed to be worried, and the sea dragon's body twisted and spiraled in the rushing wind.

"Keep straight, Master Yofune," Tanuki called out while grasping onto the reptile's horns, "I can see the ocean not too far ahead. The old tear in the Curtain should still be just off shore."

David clung with all his might to Yofune's neck. *Great, we have to go through water again to get back through the Curtain.* He was going to be waterlogged before this ordeal was over.

The land beneath them ran out and they flew over the dark waters of the ocean. Yofune lowered himself to skim across the surface, dipping his claws into his natural element.

"I'd hold your breath if I were you," Tanuki yelled back to David.

David had barely half a second to do as suggested

before Yofune dove down beneath the waves. He had to hold on with even greater strength as the water pushed against him, almost ripping him free from the dragon's back. He kept his eyes shut, hoping Yofune would resurface soon—but maybe the dragon did not realize that being human, David was likely to drown.

But then he found that he could breathe just fine.

Opening his eyes, they were no longer surrounded by the murky depths, but they were traversing through the fog of the Curtain. There was nothing to see or hear at first, but then Yofune landed, skidding on his belly for a minute or two before coming to a stop.

Tanuki lost his grip on Yofune's horns and fell backwards, tumbling onto David's lap. He looked up at the boy, and said, "Did you lose your breakfast back there? Because I think I'm about to." Placing a paw to his mouth, he rolled off of David and plopped to the ground with the grace of a sack of rice.

Yofune turned this way and that in the fog, sniffing the air. "I can smell the scent of your friend and his odd herbs ... plus the smells of many others ...but the scent is very faint. There were people here, but they have been gone for a long while."

David looked around, and saw large rectangular shapes in the Curtain's fog. He knew they were the caravan wagons that Acacia had left behind when they all went to the Sirens' Festival.

"This is where Acacia left the rest of the caravan," he

told Yofune. "We mustn't be too far from the home of the sirens." A quick thought struck him. "I have something in one of the wagons that should help."

The boy, dragon and badger approached the wagons, and David entered each one, rummaging through things. What he wanted was his dagger. He wasn't sure if it had been discarded that night when he had been captured, but he assumed the gypsies kept it, if only to resell it. Any weapon would be helpful if he was going to encounter whatever beast Nico had in his employment.

He went into Gullin's wagon, his hopes high. If anyone would have held onto his dagger, it would be Gullin, having once been a Master Huntsman. He went to the large wooden chest in the corner, and sure enough, inside of it was David's sheathed blade.

There was a whole array of hunting weapons in the chest. Apparently, Gullin was still a hunter at heart. There were exotic weapons that were unfamiliar to David: a bow with a quiver of iron arrows, each with strange markings engraved into the shafts; a rusty musket with a mirror welded to the side; pouches of various herb pellets and vials of multi-colored liquids; and a foot-long metal tube with open-mouthed dogs' heads forged on each end. David stuck his dagger and the odd tube in his belt, and took the bow and arrows, since he had practiced archery for a short time with his father. The musket, while it would have been ideal, was empty of ammunition, and there was none in the chest.

He returned to his party. Tanuki twitched his nose at David's new equipment. "Boy, a samurai you are not. Leave any dirty work to me and my master."

"This isn't your fight," David noted.

"In your world, there is a justice system that punishes those who commit wrongs," Yofune said. "Do you think we have no concept of justice in our world, Sandoval-san? There has been a transgression made here, a transgression that threatens the lives of innocents. Those with the power to protect should do what they can to fight the cowards who do evil."

This is just like something out of a hero's legend. David felt a sense of empowerment flow through him at Yofune's words. "You're right. I can protect, and I can fight. Nico is the coward, and I personally want to set him in his place."

A toothy smile spread over Yofune's face. "You are brave, but naive. You wish to protect because you believe that you are good, and that good is stronger than evil. It is not always, young man. Many times, many suffer at evil hands, for centuries …" The dragon sighed, as one of his claws touched the scars around his eyes, "… before justice is finally dealt. I confess, I am not good at heart. I have devoured thousands without thought or remorse. One day, a young woman exacted revenge, taking my sight. Only then were my eyes truly opened. I see that weakness is not in those who are victims, but in those who victimize others. I will not tolerate such cruelty

127

anymore." His face hardened. "Be warned, Sandoval-san. To stop the merciless, even a pure heart must be willing to show no mercy. Do you understand?"

David stood a moment, taking in Yofune's story. "I do," he replied. He wouldn't mind kicking in Nico's teeth if the chance presented itself.

"Hey, this is nice and comfy." Tanuki's voice was coming from the open wagon which held Acacia's cushion-filled nest. The badger snuggled up against the soft pillows. "Someone knows how to live. Is this pure silk?" He dug himself down under the cushions. "It's nice and cool down here," he added, his voice muffled. "These would be great for my burrow."

"Get out of there!" David ordered as he walked over to the bowl. "That is Acacia's bed! You have no right to dig around in it."

"There's something lumpy down here," came the muffled voice again. Tanuki popped back up from the cushions, a viola in his paws. "Why does the sphinx sleep on top of such pointy stuff?"

The viola threw David into confusion. "How on earth … but that's impossible. I destroyed that viola. How could Acacia have …" His curiosity drove him to pull up a few of the cushions. As he went deeper, he found more: violins, harps, lutes, lyres, a mandolin, and even a cello. Some of them were brand new, some chipped and splintered, some with only one string left. There was an entire string section of an orchestra in the bowl.

Why does she have these? He wondered. Was it coincidental that she horded instruments, and he had known how to play one? Or was there something more to this musical collection, particularly that they all were members of the string family?

He pressed his fingers onto the viola. He strummed one of the strings, and a velvety ping resounded from it.

I can tell, with those fine fingers of yours, you'll be an excellent musician …

He pulled back his hand as if the viola had just given him an electric shock.

Yofune peered into the nest at David's findings. "Sphinxes have curious fascinations," he said. "But we are wasting time. Come, Tanuki, you may play later. Now that I have the sphinx's scent, we should be able to find her quickly."

The badger moaned in disappointment as he ambled out of the bowl and back onto the top of Yofune's head. David again climbed up onto Yofune's back, gripping the bow and quiver of arrows slung over his shoulder. The dragon took a deep inhale of the nest, memorizing Acacia's smell, and he was off again, whipping through the Curtain like a roaring wind off the sea.

The fog dissipated gradually, but traces of it hung in the air as David noticed that they were flying through a dark, gurgling marshland. The trees loomed tall around them, creating a canopy above that blocked out the sky, making it hard to tell if it was daytime or night. The water around them was viscous with algae, and shaggy patches of peat popped up here and there in the mud. It was unsettlingly still, except for the occasional sounds of bullfrogs and night birds.

"Yofune, this is not the right place," David said. "This is not the island of the sirens."

The badger shushed David, bringing his paw to his lips. The dragon curled his neck around and spoke softly. "The Teumessian would not have been so foolish as to hold your sphinx's family captive in a place that is so easily accessible to anyone on this side of the Curtain. Undoubtedly, the sirens summoned help to the island to rescue your friends. He has taken them to a hidden place, where he can mask the humans' scent and leave no trail behind. Fortunately for us, it is a place that the sphinx must know about, for I smell her presence here. She cannot be far ahead of us."

Or this is a place that Nico has led her to, as a trap, David thought.

Yofune landed on a damp mound of dirt, in which there was a large hole that led down into the earth. It was big enough that Yofune could enter, but there was no indication of how far down it went.

"A foxhole," Tanuki confirmed. "I mean, it would have to be a fox the size of the Umibozu, but I can tell that kind of digging work anywhere. Not as beautiful as a badger burrow."

Yofune sniffed down into the hole, but jerked his

head back. A deep, deadly growl emitted from his throat.

"What is it, Master?" Tanuki ventured to ask, gripping tightly to Yofune's antler.

"There is another scent down there, one I know well," Yofune replied tensely. "This 'monster' that aids the Teumessian is a shunned member of the dragon clans."

David's eyes widened. "Another dragon?"

Yofune nodded solemnly. "The Sleepless Dragon of Colchis. He was once charged with protecting an ancient golden fleece, but then a human warrior used a potion on him that charmed him to sleep. The human stole the sacred fleece, and ever since the Sleepless Dragon has vowed never to be tricked again. He stole a charm that prevents him from ever sleeping. He feeds on the resentment and hatred in his heart. The rest of dragon society has exiled him. If the fox has put him in charge and he is staying on guard down there, he will be relentless. He will not be easily defeated again."

David thought back to the story of the Argonaut Jason and the Colchian Dragon, a myth he knew well. "But I thought Jason killed the dragon after he put it to sleep," he said.

Yofune huffed a laugh. "It sounds more heroic to say you slew a fearsome beast, rather than say you lulled it to sleep and then ran for your dear little life."

The young man sucked in his breath. The Sleepless Dragon must be the monster that Gullin was talking about. Gullin, one of the Master Huntsmen, rumored to be the greatest order of beast slayers on earth, had been overcome by this adversary. And Acacia was down there somewhere, ready to fight it to save her family. If it was true that the Sleepless Dragon could no longer be charmed to sleep, her hypnotic powers would be of no use. If Nico was also down there, who knew what other traps or tricks he might have lying in wait.

David let out his breath, grasping his bow firmly in his hands. "We need to go down there. I'm ready if you are."

Yofune made a nod of agreement, then turned and started down into the darkness of the foxhole.

Tanuki gulped, and meekly said in the dark, "I don't suppose we could go back to that nice bed with the silk cushions? I'd rather die there than down in this hole …"

CHAPTER NINE

Darkness congested every inch of the tunnel as Yofune descended deeper and deeper underground. The surrounding blackness mattered little to the sea dragon, whose blindness only made his other senses more acute. Tanuki could see well enough in the dark, although he whispered to David that there was not much to see other than dirt and a few twisted roots in the tunnel walls. David felt suspended in the darkness, and this made their descent feel as if it was killing hour after hour, although he knew in reality that perhaps twenty minutes or so had passed.

A faint glow flickered down below them, a warm ripple that teased them to come closer. David poured all of his focus onto that light, both grateful for a reprieve from the darkness and anxious about what the light would reveal.

What awaited them at the end of the tunnel caught them by surprise.

Before them was a grand Victorian mansion, nearly a castle in stature, abundant in steeples and gables and lit with hundreds of ornate oil lamps all around its perimeter. It was a majestic marvel of architecture buried like the greatest treasure underground. In front of this luxurious abode, a battle was ensuing, between a ferocious flying sphinx and a gigantic dark-green reptile ten times her size.

The dragon was bloated and arthritic with age, a mere shadow of the sleek scaled guardian depicted in the old paintings. While it was much slower than the sphinx that darted with ease around its head, the colossal beast was immovable. He had planted himself directly at the entrance to the mansion, his backside blocking the front doors, which were the only entryway. His ragged wings created gusts of wind to drive away his opponent. He snapped his great jaws and belched forth fire, which the sphinx dodged as she fought back with claw and tooth. She inhaled deeply and released her serenity-inducing breath, but the dragon retaliated with his own breath, a thick noxious fume of smoke and sulfur. Acacia hacked and coughed as the poisonous smell clouded her face. The distraction was enough for the dragon to smack her out of the air with a brutal swat of his hand.

"Acacia!" David hollered. He readied an iron arrow in his bow to shoot.

"Put your weapon away," Yofune ordered. "It will do no good. The strongest of metals cannot penetrate his scales, which is how he has survived all these years."

The Sleepless Dragon finally noticed this new group

of trespassers. He placed one of his great claws on the prone sphinx's back, pinning her down. He flashed his stalagmite-sharp fangs at them, and roared a deadly threat.

"Enough of this foolishness," Yofune roared back at his draconic brethren. "The sphinx is not your enemy. You are holding innocent lives hostage at the behest of a scoundrel. Do not shame yourself further with this ridiculousness."

The Sleepless Dragon scowled at Yofune Nushi. "I remember you," he sneered. "You are the one who was blinded by a human girl. I have no fear of you." He twisted his claw into Acacia's skin, not hard enough to pierce it but enough to cause pain. She winced, trying to free herself from his grasp.

Yofune reared up onto his back legs. "I don't need my sight to deal with you. I will ask one last time for you to leave, and retain what little dignity you may have left."

"Spare me your nonsense," the Sleepless Dragon retorted. "I have been charged to guard this place and let no one through. I can redeem myself after my failure all those centuries ago. I will not be deprived of the chance to reclaim my honor, Blind One, not even by you."

One of Yofune's scaly eyebrows rose up. "What exactly do you owe the Teumessian, that you agreed to this scheme?"

The bloated old dragon snorted in contempt. "I do not owe my grand-nephew anything. I have more love for him than my grand-niece. She is against me like the rest. Only Nico understands my plight."

David wiped a hand over his face. This Sleepless Dragon was Acacia and Nico's grand-uncle? Was everyone on this side of the Curtain related?

"Dismount," Yofune hissed in a low voice to David and Tanuki. The two readily complied as Yofune lowered his head to the ground. "I will get him away from the door. You and the sphinx will only have a few seconds to get past him. Be sure you are ready."

"Yes, sir," David whispered back. Tanuki gulped.

The Sleepless Dragon lowered his head, glaring at David and Tanuki. "So tiny and frail," he snarled. "I would rather not crush you, but I will have no choice if you come any closer."

"It is not with them that you should concern yourself," Yofune growled. With terrifying speed, he launched himself at the Sleepless Dragon.

In a blur of blue and green, the two dragons were locked in a battle that shook the entire cavern, threatening to bring the whole underground lair crumbling down. Yofune tossed the Sleepless Dragon to the side, freeing Acacia from his clutches. The Japanese sea dragon coiled around his opponent like a python, digging his fangs into the monster's snout. The Sleepless Dragon howled, madly spitting fire like the Gates of Hell, pushing against Yofune's coils with titanic strength.

David and Tanuki rushed over to Acacia, helping her up onto her feet. "We have to go inside now, while we have the chance," David said.

The sphinx nodded.

Before they could get to the doors of the mansion, a massive green tail slammed down in front of them. Had they been half a second faster, the tail would have crushed them.

The Sleepless Dragon untwisted Yofune from his body and slammed him against the ground, causing an earth-quaking rumble. He snapped his head around to look at David and his friends with fiery, mad eyes. "No one is getting past me this time!" He inhaled to breathe a fiery blaze at them, but an intense blast of icy water smacked him in the face.

David let out a heavy exhale of relief. He should have figured that Yofune had water breath.

The force of the water blast forced the Sleepless Dragon to twist away and lose sight of his prey. Yofune continued his water attack as the three jumped over the tail, dashed up the steps of the mansion, across the porch and to the doors …

To find them locked.

"*Maldito!*" David hissed, pulling and shoving with all his might against the doors.

"Ahem, allow me," Tanuki said, patting David on the leg. The badger inflated to the size and musculature of a gorilla. With one mighty swing of his arm, he smashed the doors clean open. They all ran inside and down into the mysterious, dark hallway.

Once they were out of sight of the front door, the three carefully made their way through the halls of the mansion. Acacia sniffed around each corner, claws at the ready for whatever may jump out at them. Tanuki fussed that his paw hurt from knocking open the doors.

"You know, you could have turned into a key to open the doors," David remarked.

"But where's the fun in that?" the badger replied, rubbing his paw. "I hope Master will be okay out there against that big meanie. Ow, ow, ow …"

David noticed how the tremors from the dragons' battle had ceased. He hoped that it was a good sign, and that Yofune had won. He noticed Acacia was giving him a concerned look. It was because he was holding onto one of her wings. He hadn't realized he had grabbed it. He quickly let it go.

"Are you all right?" he asked. "Did he hurt you badly?"

Acacia shook her head. She continued down the hallway, determination in every step.

They came to a pair of finely carved marble doors, white and speckled with black. David warily pushed at the doors' handles, and the doors opened with ease. Acacia grabbed him by the shoulder, pushing him back as she inspected the entryway, sniffing and clawing carefully at the doorframe. A low growl rolled from her throat, a warning to any enemies that may be lurking behind the doors.

David could understand her uneasiness. An open door was a sure sign of a trap. "Do you smell or sense anything?" he asked.

Acacia crinkled her nose and snarled. Her claws flexed, and she swished her tail from side to side.

"Nico has been here?" David surmised.

She nodded.

"Do you think he's in there now?"

She shook her head.

David knew they shouldn't take any chances. "Tanuki, can you make yourself very small, and sneak around a bit?" he asked. "To make sure there aren't any traps."

The badger crossed his arms, sighing. "Of course, send the badger in to be the bait. 'Tanuki, could you stick your paw in this bear trap, and see if it works?' Honestly, I have to do everything around here."

Tanuki turned himself into a small cloud and wafted into the ballroom. He gently breezed past wall paintings, traced along the floor, and floated up to the large crystal chandelier. After a minute of inspection, he returned to the group and resumed his badger shape.

"Seems safe to me," he reported.

David readied an arrow in his bow, and he stepped into the room. Acacia walked side by side with David, her smirk hinting that she was intrigued by the boy's warrior-like attentiveness. They crossed the ballroom floor, their reflections visible in the polished surface.

They made it all the way across the room to another pair of doors on the other side. These doors were made of the same speckled marble. Acacia sniffed at the doors, and instantly grew excited. She scratched and shoved at the doors with all of her might, growing increasingly frenzied. She threw her body against them, trying to knock them down.

"What is it?" David asked, placing a hand on her shoulder to stop her from hurting herself. "Do you smell your family? Are they on the other side?"

Acacia nodded vigorously.

"Stand aside, puny ones," Tanuki stated, apparently having gotten over his sore paw. "Let the most divine being in Kyoto handle this." He bulked up again to his gorilla size. He readied his shoulders, and at full force he barreled into the marble doors. This time, however, his strength had no effect. He hit his head hard against the marble. He staggered back, blinking, and fell over onto the floor. He instantly shrank back down to normal size.

Acacia picked up the woozy badger in her arms, tenderly rubbing his head. He looked up at her, remarking, "Hey lady, did you see the cart that hit me? That guy owes me fifty yen ..."

David looked over the doors. There were no keyholes, no latches, no handles, and no hinges to take apart. Only solid marble. There was something engraved into the stone, a wheel of runic letters encircled by a wreath of tiny-leafed vines. He recognized the Celtic runes from a book of Druidism that his aunt, a rare book collector, had bought for him in Madrid. His mother had banned the "godless, unholy scribble" from the house, so David had not had the chance to understand the meanings of runes.

"There are some runes written here," he told Acacia. "But I can't understand them."

Acacia came over and looked at the inscription. She pondered, getting the same look of concentration on her face as when she was in the riddle contest with Nico. After a minute, she spoke a long string of words, in what sounded like a mixture of Latin and another language—David thought it sounded Gaelic. Despite the protection that the Latin language should have provided to subdue the Shade inside of her, she cringed in gut-searing pain. The seal of vines shimmered green, and the doors slowly opened in response to her voice.

David grimaced. Of course Nico had set a barrier that forced Acacia to speak. The runes must be a magical seal that by speaking a counter spell would open the doors. It was a trick that was designed to hurt Acacia. He prayed her family was on the other side and that would be the end of it.

But when they walked through the doors, they found themselves standing in an identical ballroom to the one they had just left.

Acacia called out in a howl, pausing to see if anyone would reply. There was no sound. She moved frantically around the room, trying to pick up the scent of her beloved gypsies. Her sense of smell led to another pair of marble doors at the other side of the room. Once again, there were no handles or keyholes or hinges. Acacia, in frustration, rammed against the doors and scratched furiously into the stone.

David and Tanuki glanced at one another, just as puzzled as the sphinx. They both cast their gaze around the room, looking for signs of how this trick had been done. When David looked behind them, he saw that the doors they had come through were closed shut, as if they had never been opened. David went back to try and push open the doors. They were frozen solid.

"That's not good," Tanuki commented bluntly.

David remembered a few of the Latin words that Acacia had used to open the doors. He tried, with the best pronunciation he could, to repeat the counter-spell so the doors might open again.

Nothing.

"We're stuck," he confirmed, resting his head against the marble.

Acacia was hissing at them, beckoning for them to come over to her. As the two approached, they saw that another set of Celtic runes had been carved into the doors. David put a hand on Acacia's arm and spoke in a low voice. "Acacia, I bet I can figure out how to speak the spell to open this door. I understand some Latin, and I read a book about runes once. Maybe I should give it a try, so the Shade doesn't hurt you—"

Acacia whipped her head around to glare at him. There was anger in her eyes, and she shook her head. He did not know if this was out of pride, or because she did not trust him to speak the spell correctly. Maybe it was mentioning the Shade of Nyx that put her on edge. She didn't want to be weak.

Or maybe, she didn't want *him* to think she was weak.

Before he could say anything else, Acacia spoke the runic spell. The doors opened with a welcoming flourish, as before. The color of Acacia's skin was growing pale, and her lips were becoming dry and cracked. But she continued on into the next room. David sighed to himself and followed.

Yet again, another ballroom. And again, a pair of marble doors at the other side.

Trails of steam drifted up from Tanuki's head. "This is pointless!" he barked angrily. "We'll be here for a thousand years at this rate."

The stress was getting to Acacia as well. She clutched her paws to her head, her teeth clenched in rage. David turned and saw the doors behind them were closed, barring them inside the room. He rubbed his chin, thinking.

"Nico has obviously put some kind of enchantment in place to make this barrier repeat itself, but how?" He tried to think of any stories he had read where the hero was put in a similar situation, but he couldn't remember how any characters had overcome this type of obstacle. There must be something in the room itself. All he could see were paintings on the walls, the candlelit sconces, and the chandelier ...

While he was thinking, Acacia stormed off to the next set of doors and was reading the expected inscription on them. David, knowing that she was going to speak again, ran over and pulled her back. "Acacia, this is exactly what Nico wants you to do! He set this trap up so you would keep talking. Your family is not on the other side of these doors. This is going to go on forever until the Shade kills you!"

David received a reaction that he did not expect. Acacia bared her teeth at him, and growled so disturbingly that it caused him to step back. Her ferocity subsided when she saw the bewildered look on his face. She placed her paws on the door, like an arrested criminal, and hung her head. Her hair draped over her face so David couldn't see her, but he thought he saw a drop of sweat fall and splash on the floor beneath her. It could have been a tear.

"Calm down, calm down," he said quietly. "We're going to figure this out. There must be something in this room that's the key. Something behind one of these paintings, maybe ..." He began to start looking behind the wall paintings, checking to see if anything was hidden beneath the wallpaper, tapping various spots along the walls. He looked back at Acacia. She was sitting on the floor, hunched over like a dog being punished. "We can't give up now. This is just like a riddle, isn't it? You're good at those. Besides, Nico could be watching us right now, so let's not give him the satisfaction of despair. Come on, get up."

David returned to Acacia, lifting her up onto her hind feet so he could look her in the eye. "Acacia, I don't know a lot about you, but I know you're strong. You've fought against that Shade inside of you. You protect your family, at the risk of your own well being. You even saved me, when you didn't have to. So, keep being strong, okay? No doubt, no giving in, no fear."

Whatever distant plane of hopelessness she had been lost in, Acacia was returning from it. She took a deep breath. She placed her paws on her stomach, curling her claws, indicating the parasitic essence inside of her. "*Nullus metus*," she said softly.

Nullus metus. No fear.

David nodded. "That's good, Acacia. Don't be afraid of the Shade. We're going to get rid of it. You'll be fine."

She took his face in her paws, holding him as one would cradle a sacred relic. She gazed deeply into his eyes. Then, very softly, very slowly, she spoke. "I am sorry …what I've done …"

It was the first time he had heard her speak his language. It was somehow even more beautiful than her dream voice. Instantly, however, her speaking triggered the Shade inside of her, and it had a more rapid effect on her than before. She gasped as something greenish-blue in color swam through her veins, the sickening shade visible through her skin.

"Acacia, don't!" David demanded. "You're only going to—"

She put her paw over his lips to hush him. "I am not afraid … of what lies inside me. I … promised myself … I would speak with my own voice … to say this." She steadied herself, as the poisonous Shade poured more heavily through her body. "I thought … when you found me … you … were one I was supposed to find. I was told … about a vision … and I hoped it meant you … but I cannot … put you through more … grief … David, I … don't want you to … be hurt … I—"

By now, Acacia's skin had turned nearly paint-white as the Shade sucked the color out of her. She was withering away before David's eyes. As she gasped and coughed, her tongue turned a nasty green. Even her hair was changing from its rich dark brunette to smoky gray. Her hands dropped lifelessly to her sides. Her eyes rolled back in her head.

"No, no!" David wrapped his arms around Acacia as her body crumpled over. She was growing feral, the pain causing her to gnash her teeth and hiss and spit like an enraged cat.

Tanuki backed away. "That's very bad, David!

Grandpa Raiju started acting like that right before—"
He morphed back into a cloud and floated up to hide up
inside the chandelier.

David could only think of one thing to do. He
reached into his pocket and pulled out Gullin's pouch of
herb pellets. He didn't know what medicinal value they
had, but he had nothing else on him. He took out one
of the pellets and managed to get it into Acacia's mouth.
He kept his hand over her lips so she wouldn't spit it out,
and she swallowed it. She gradually stopped thrashing
about as the pellet induced a calmness within her. She
still looked terrible, but the pain that the Shade was
causing was subsiding for the moment. Acacia looked
up at David, the gold of her eyes faded to yellow. She
rubbed her head against his shoulder, purring weakly.

"We're going to be all right," David promised. "We're
going to find your family, get out of here, and then I'm
going to find out how to get that Shade out of you. But
please … don't talk anymore for now."

"Do chandeliers normally have mirrors in them?"
Tanuki called out from his hiding place. "That's odd,
don't you think?"

David looked up at him. "A mirror?"

Tanuki poked his head out from the crystal
chandelier. "Yes, it's pointing face down. See?"

David set Acacia down gently for her to rest on
the floor. He stood and walked directly under the
chandelier, and sure enough, he could see a small mirror

facing down at him. It was about the size of a tea saucer, and it was angled so that one could only have seen it by standing where David was now. "Can you bring that mirror down here?" he called.

After a minute, Tanuki called back, "Nope, it's welded on here. It won't budge."

That was curious. David contemplated as his gaze wandered down to the floor. The highly reflective floor that mimicked his image like a mirror. A mirror above him, and one below him …

"That's how Nico did it!" he confirmed. "He's got two mirrors facing one another."

"Huh?" the badger squeaked.

"If you've got two mirrors facing one another, the reflections in each one go on forever," David explained. "That's why this room keeps repeating itself over and over. It's a never-ending reflection!"

"Oh, I knew that," Tanuki replied. "Well, let's get rid of this then. It might take me a little while, but I'll chew through this chandelier's cord—"

"We don't have a little while. We need to get Acacia out of here right now!" David readied his bow and pointed an arrow straight up at the mirror above him. He let the arrow fly just as Tanuki was calling, "Let me get down from here first!!"

The arrow impaled the mirror dead center, shattering it instantly. It released a burst of blue energy that made the whole chandelier combust. Tanuki was flung through the air in a shower of glass. The whole structure came plummeting down, and David jumped and rolled out of the way before it crashed on the ballroom floor, sprinkling crystal shards everywhere.

A feather gently glided down to the floor, before it popped back into the familiar form of Tanuki. The badger chattered angrily at David in an animal language that David couldn't understand. "Idiot," Tanuki finished under his breath.

With the mirror shattered, the marble doors at both ends of the room creaked open. Through the doors where Acacia was lying, they could see the three stolen caravan wagons at the far end of a dimly lit corridor.

Acacia bolted to her feet, but she stumbled in exhaustion. David dashed over to help her, and this time she accepted his assistance. He put his arm around her middle to hold her steady. They walked out of the ballroom and down the corridor with Tanuki scuttling after them.

David glanced over at Acacia, glad to see that the color was returning to her face. "Are you feeling any better?" he asked.

Acacia smiled at him, and pressed her forehead against his.

David smiled back. "Let's go free your family."

CHAPTER TEN

The three wagons stood patiently as the rescuers approached. There were heavy inch-thick chains with iron padlocks enveloping each wagon in criss-crossing webs, making it impossible for anything to get in or out. Tanuki transformed into a skeleton key, zipping through the air and unlocking every padlock. Acacia pulled the clanking chains away and yanked down the walls of each wagon with surprising strength, given her condition.

The gypsies had been crammed together inside the wagons, without any light or space. They flooded out of the wagons with shouts of joy, crowding around Acacia in a mass of embraces. Gullin swept up Acacia in his arms and gave her a mighty hug, and she nuzzled his cheek. The Scotsman placed her down and gave David a hearty slap on the back.

"Knew you'd come through for us, boyo," he laughed. "Sorry I missed out on the fun."

"I'm not sure if the 'fun' is done yet," David replied. "We still need to get out of here."

"Good point. I see you brought a few of my 'special

girls.' " Gullin looked over the hunting weapons David had brought. He plucked the dog-headed metal tube from David's belt. "Ah, you brought good ol' Orthrus. You have good taste, lad. Don't mind if I keep her warm for now?" He stuck "Orthrus" in his own belt.

"Well, it's your … stick," David answered.

"Is that gopher with you?" Gullin asked, gesturing at Tanuki, who poked his head out from behind David's legs.

Tanuki cocked his head to the side. "Is he talking about me?" he asked. "Is he saying how marvelous I am?"

Gullin blinked in curiosity at the talking animal. "Heh, it talks, eh? Can't understand a bloody thing it's saying."

At first, David was confused as to why Gullin and Tanuki could not understand what each other was saying. Then he remembered that Tanuki spoke Japanese and not English, and Gullin was the other way around. It was because of the kappa's mystical waters that David could understand Japanese. It hadn't occurred to him that he was automatically switching back and forth between the two languages, depending on who he was talking to.

"This is Tanuki. He's been a big help to us," David told Gullin. "He can change into different shapes."

Gullin scratched his beard. "I don't trust those shape-shifting types. Dirty little tricksters, the lot of 'em."

David looked down at Tanuki. "Gullin says you're the most brilliant animal he's ever seen."

Tanuki beamed.

"But right now, I need you to turn into something that can carry us all out of here and back to someplace safe," David said.

Tanuki frowned. "Even the most divine being in all Kyoto has his limits. I haven't figured out how to turn into anything larger than a human on horseback yet. Everyone here can walk, can't they?"

"But it'll take us forever to climb up out of this cavern and through the swamp to get back through the Curtain on foot. We better go find Master Yofune."

"That's going to be a bit of a problem," interjected a voice as dark and slick as oil.

Everyone turned to see Nico standing in the doorway at the end of the corridor. He was dressed in a garish blue suit, which accentuated the bright orange of his hair and wickedly-gleaming eyes.

"Honestly, I leave for a short while, and you disobedient pets get out of your cages?" He shook his finger at them, clicking his tongue. "Clearly your former owner didn't train you properly."

Acacia flexed her claws, preparing to bolt straight at her canine cousin, but Gullin beat her to it. As the Huntsman came within range and raised his fist, the fox leapt, somersaulting over Gullin's head. He landed lightly on the ground behind Gullin, who pivoted back around to attempt another strike. Nico glided sideways and catapulted himself at the man, striking him in the shoulder. Gullin twisted backwards from the blow and landed heavily on his back. Nico took hold of him by the leg, swung him around and released. Gullin flew across the corridor before colliding into David's legs, bowling him over.

Nico casually dusted off his coat, not having broken a sweat. "You may have muscle, but my bloodline has been blessed with the fortune to never be caught. Don't embarrass yourself."

Acacia started to charge at Nico, but she faltered. She clutched her stomach, feeling the burning of the Shade in her blood and organs. Her resolve drove her forward, her teeth and claws bared for shredding. She stopped when Nico began laughing hysterically, wiping a tear from his eye.

"My goodness, Cousin," he chortled. "This is the most pathetic thing I've ever seen. The mighty sphinx, thinking she can protect her pride, and she looks like a withered old tabby. Even I would feel guilty fighting you. Go on, run along now, kitty. I'll take care of your filthy little brood. I'll even be nice to your favorite, and make him my personal servant."

Murder filled Acacia's eyes. She wouldn't let this horrid poison inside defeat her, and she sure as Hades wasn't going to let Nico get away with this! She summoned all of her strength to attack, but then she heard the tightening of a bow string. David was aiming an arrow right at Nico. Gullin stood up, his arms up in a fighter's pose. Behind them, the rest of the gypsies banded together into a tight formation, angry faces all focused on Nico.

"You hurt her," Gullin bellowed, "and you'll be little more than a mess of bloody fur and broken bone!"

Nico sighed, and stepped backwards into the ballroom. "I'm beginning to think you pets aren't worth the trouble," he remarked. With a few quick words of Latin, he commanded the ballroom doors to slam shut.

"Don't let that mongrel get away!" Gullin ordered. The group rushed towards the doors.

Alarm rang in David's mind. "Wait! Stop! This could be a—"

The doors flung open as the gypsies reached them, and the walls peeled back and disintegrated. They were standing on the front veranda of the mansion, and right in front of them was the gaping mouth of the Sleepless Dragon.

Everyone froze, paralyzed with fear. Acacia extended her wings wide to shield the others and ushered them away from the monster. Gullin planted his feet firmly, removing Orthrus from his belt. "Aye, I owe you for the last time, you fat lizard! Come at me, then!"

The Sleepless Dragon did not hesitate. His massive maw shot down at Gullin, ready to ingest the man. Gullin placed his fingers on the two dog heads on each end of Orthrus, and twisted subtly. There was a soft click, and out from the dogs' mouths extended a collapsible staff. Sliding like a telescope, it elongated to eight feet in length. As the dragon's teeth were closing in over Gullin's head, he jammed the staff into the beast's mouth, locking its jaw in place. The dragon reared its head back with a furious roar, and Gullin held onto his staff, carried upwards inside the dragon's jaws.

"Now, boyo!" he called down to David. "The only way to wound a beast like this is from the inside! Shoot an arrow into the roof of its mouth, into the brain!" Gullin punched the dragon in the gums with his bare fist, and broke the tip of one of the teeth.

David readied his bow, but the dragon was thrashing about too wildly for him to get a clear shot. He saw a faint light in the dragon's throat, and he knew it was a fireball igniting.

"Tanuki! Go up there and give Gullin my dagger!" he ordered, yanking his dagger out of its sheath.

The badger looked at David blankly. "You must be joking."

"That dragon is about to fry Gullin. You can turn into a rain cloud to douse the fire. Please, Tanuki, I need your help!"

The badger twitched his whiskers nervously, but he took David's dagger from him. "You owe me soooooooooo much sake for this."

Tanuki turned into a pouring rain cloud, and he

whisked up to the dragon's mouth. Steam immediately began filling the air as the heat from the Sleepless Dragon's gullet clashed with the cold rainwater from Tanuki's cloud. The cloud dropped the dagger into Gullin's hand, but at that moment, Orthrus collapsed under the pressure of the dragon's crushing jaws.

The dragon's mouth snapped shut. It swallowed.

David, Acacia and the gypsies were petrified. Acacia's bestial cry of rage brought everything back into motion. She pumped her wings, leaping up to pulverize her grand-uncle. David caught her hind leg in mid-air, struggling to keep her earthbound.

"Acacia, stop!" he cried. "He'll kill you too—"

They heard the sound of distant thunder.

The Sleepless Dragon's eyes shot wide open, and his jaw dropped. The thunder grew louder. The dragon looked down at his belly. A faint light flickered under his skin.

David had often mused on how dragons could breathe fire when he read stories about Saint George or Sir Lancelot. One theory he had devised was that they store gas in their stomachs from the breakdown of food, and when it passes through the lungs, it mixes with various chemicals and ignites upon exhalation. If his theory was to be believed—taking into account that dragon gas would be extremely flammable—then a dragon that has swallowed a creature capable of generating lightning would be an explosion waiting to happen.

This was no exception.

Fire and lightning erupted from the dragon in a deafening blast, with such volcanic intensity that it burst his stomach straight through his skin. The Sleepless Dragon crashed to the earth, shaking the foundations of the mansion. The charred carcass smoked, and a syrupy black goo leaked from the lifeless mouth.

The dragon would never be sleepless again.

There was little to be joyous about, however. The gypsies, the sphinx and David stared at the scorched mess of reptile.

Tanuki …Gullin… David felt a part of him ripped asunder. *They sacrificed themselves to save the rest of us.*

The dragon's underside twitched. The gypsies retreated away with shouts of warning, pointing at the shifting skin. Acacia and David held their breaths as something tumbled out from the burnt gap where the dragon's stomach had burst through. It looked like a treasure chest made of solid stone, and coated in a thick putrid ooze that smoked. Once the chest plunked down on the ground, the lid popped open. Out of it arose Gullin, plastered in the smelly goo, but unharmed. Then the chest changed into the shape of Tanuki, who caught his breath and looked as frazzled as a chicken that had escaped the cooking pot.

A wild cheer erupted from the group. In unison, they dashed over to the valiant dragon slayers. They used scarves and bits of clothing to wipe the hunter and the badger clean.

Gullin walked over to David, handing him back the dagger. "Thanks for lending it to me, boyo. But blowing a dragon up from the inside out was more fun than sticking it in the brain." He glanced at the badger, who was blissfully being tended to by two of the gypsy girls. "I have to admit, that gopher's a clever little lad. Changed into that box just in time before we got blown to high heaven."

David kneeled down and helped wipe Tanuki clean with the arm cuff of his shirt. "Gullin called you clever, for that trick you did by turning into a box."

Tanuki snorted. "Clever, right. If I was so clever, I would have blown up that fat toad before he fought Master Yofune ..." He sniffled, wiping his nose. "Poor Master. I was supposed to look after him."

Only now did David realize that Master Yofune was nowhere to be found. If the Sleepless Dragon survived the earlier fight ...

"Stop your sniffling." Punctually in response to Tanuki's woe, Yofune glided through the air towards them, battle-worn and exhausted. "I appreciate the concern, but give an old dragon credit."

"Master!" The badger scurried over to his giant lord and hugged one of his great scaled forelegs.

The gypsies reeled back, clutching at one another in fright. Gullin grabbed the bow and arrows off David's shoulder, slipping an arrow into place with quick precision. "Not another one! This one doesn't look too tough—"

David grabbed Gullin by his wrist. "No! Gullin, this is Yofune Nushi. He's a friend. He brought me here to find everyone."

Acacia cooed in agreement.

Gullin lowered the bow. "I suppose you can understand what that one is saying too?" he asked.

"It's Japanese. I'll teach you sometime," David answered with a wry grin. He turned back to Yofune. "What happened? We thought you were—"

"Deceived, is all," Yofune replied. "In the middle of our battle, the coward slipped off out of my reach. The air became full with an awful musk, and I could no longer smell my adversary. The scent was a mix of fox and human, but also an absurd cologne. I don't know this Teumessian of yours well, but I believed it to be the scoundrel we were looking for. I tracked him up out of the den and through the swamp. He took me for a long pursuit, until I finally found the source of the scent." Yofune curled back his lips to show a silken ascot between his teeth. "The fox-man used this as a decoy to lure me away, to leave you defenseless. By then I realized the trick and turned around to return here, but he left strong smells planted everywhere to confuse me."

David clenched his fists. How was Nico always one step ahead of them? He probably had more allies than they knew, helping him with these schemes. Then again, the Teumessian had said he was blessed with the ability to never be caught. Was there some truth to that?

"I'm glad you are all right," David replied, calming himself down. "Are you strong enough to carry us out of here?"

The sea dragon stood on wobbly legs, but he nodded. "I should have enough strength left for the task. If Tanuki would be so kind as to take some of the burden off my claws."

Tanuki nodded happily. "Of course, master! One moment." The badger concentrated deeply, and shifted into the form of a large horse. "I'm afraid this is the best I can do," he apologized. "I'm tired too, after blowing up a dragon and all."

Tanuki was hitched to one of the wagons, while the other two were strapped to Yofune's long winding body. Being fatigued and weighed down by the wagons and their occupants, Yofune could not manage enough strength to fly, but he could walk well enough. David took the coachman's seat on the wagon that Tanuki pulled, while Gullin rode on Yofune's shoulders. This way, they could also keep an eye out for traps along the way. Despite her weak condition, Acacia chose to walk beside Tanuki rather than ride. The group began its procession out of the cavern towards the tunnel leading out.

Something behind them burst.

David snapped his head around to look back. One of the oil lamps in front of the mansion had exploded, and the flame inside was growing. The fire took on a narrow face, with two yellow eyes and two pointed ears. The hundreds of other lamps encircling the mansion blew open in succession, each with a horrible face forming in the fire. Each fire evolved into full form, with sleek bodies and blazing tails. They looked like foxes from the depths of the brimstone-laden underworld.

The fire foxes leapt from their lamp posts and chased after them.

Yofune, Tanuki and Acacia raced as fast as they could with wagons and passengers in tow, fleeing for the tunnel as the fire foxes closed in behind them.

"What are those things?" David shouted.

"Will o' Wisps," Gullin called back to him through the rush of wind. "But these ones have been corrupted. All their joy has been replaced by hatred. Guess whose work that is?"

David grabbed the reins and beckoned Tanuki to get closer to Yofune. He shouted to the dragon at the top of his voice. "Yofune, use your water breath on them!"

The sea dragon did not even look back, but kept racing. "I am out of it. I can only hold enough water at a time for three blasts, and I used them in the battle. If we can get up to the swamp, I can drink the water there to refill."

161

The foxes pursued them with the burning speed of a forest fire. David sensed that the tunnel had grown longer and steeper, or maybe it seemed that way because of their urgency to escape. The chase came to an abrupt halt as Yofune smacked hard into an unseen barrier, his body crumpling in from the harsh impact. The wagons lurched and bounced off the ground, and the gypsies inside screamed from the tumult. Tanuki dug his hooves into the damp dirt as best he could to stop, but he collided with Yofune's tail. The jolt was strong enough to throw David from his seat. He landed on Tanuki's back, rolled off and hit the ground.

Yofune, almost knocked unconscious from the impact, clutched at the ground to keep from sliding back down the tunnel. He swung his head up and rammed his antlers against the barrier, to no effect. Acacia flew to the front of the line to find out what the obstruction was. She breathed a stream of her warm breath, which clouded up on a flat surface in front of her. She scratched at it with her claws, creating a high pitched whine. It was a glass wall, but unlike any glass David had ever seen, or in this case, could not see. He climbed his way up the tunnel to the wall, throwing his weight against it. Acacia and Yofune hammered into it as well, but nothing was giving. They scanned the wall for a magical seal, similar to the one that the mansion's ballroom doors had, but there was none. David shouted out a few Latin words—"open," "vanish," "remove," and "banish." Absolutely nothing.

He knew the fire foxes would catch up to them quickly, but David examined the wall more closely. He observed that his reflection, as well as the others', was not perceptible in the glass wall, but that the tunnel behind them was reflected with sharp clarity.

"Another enchanted mirror," he wheezed. Nico must have put it in place right after Yofune came back down the tunnel after chasing him around the swamp.

Gullin, who had become tangled up in Yofune's coils upon impact, freed himself and ran over to join the others by the wall. "Boyo, use the arrows! This is magic, and the arrowheads are iron. Iron works against magic. We should be able to shoot through it." He looked back, and saw the mass of fire foxes approaching swiftly. "You handle the wall. I'll take care of those hell hounds."

David wasn't sure how Gullin intended to do that, but the sooner they got through this glass wall, the better. He strung an arrow in his bow and shot the mirror at point blank range, but it absorbed the arrow and shot it back. The arrow whooshed past David's ear and struck the frame of one of the wagons, thankfully not hurting anyone.

Acacia grabbed David's arm, shaking her head frantically. David saw that he had nicked the mirror, not much more than a sliver's breadth, but the iron had been effective. He had to try again; his last few arrows would surely break the mirror.

Meanwhile, the searing heat and smothering smoke

from the fire foxes was stripping breathable air from the tunnel. Tanuki transformed into a storm cloud, spraying the foxes with rain and hail. Gullin swung Orthrus left and right to beat the encroaching fire wisps, stamping them into smoldering embers. Several of the braver gypsies sprinted out from the wagons, with blankets and brooms and whatever they could find to smother out the fire. The fight was rapidly growing futile; the fire foxes wouldn't stay put to be snuffed out. They darted about, eating at the blankets and brooms and reducing them to ash. The gypsies were overwhelmed and suffocating, trapped in a living inferno.

David took one of the arrows from his quiver and slammed the iron tip into the tiny crack in the wall. He dug the arrowhead in repeatedly, and the crack was gradually getting bigger. At such a slow rate, however, they would be roasted by the Will O' Wisps before they could escape.

"Acacia, take the other arrow I have and help me—" When David looked over, Acacia was not beside him anymore. He searched for her until he saw her walking back towards the crackling congregation of foxes. She possessed a fixed calmness, and he couldn't imagine what she was planning to do.

Fire licked hungrily at the gypsies' clothing and skin. The heat was causing Tanuki to evaporate, and he was forced to resume badger form to avoid disappearing. The gypsies gasped and coughed for air as the foxes surged forward, eager to have their victims burn alive. The shadow of a figure intervened, halting the minions of flame from advancing further. Two black wings expanded out, taking in the heat and ash, shielding everyone behind her.

The sphinx's eyes glimmered red in the presence of the fire. Both sides stared down each other, one feline warrior against the army of canine demons. Cinders stung Acacia's face, but her expression was unwavering, cold and merciless. She stood on her hind legs, tall and proud, and placed her front paws together, claws pointed upwards.

Very, very quietly, she started speaking.

Her voice was so low, David did not know at first that she was talking. Yofune's ears picked up the sound, and his blind eyes widened. "Oh dear …" he whispered. His voice suddenly boomed over the popping crackle of the foxes' flames. "David! Tanuki! You must come here! All of you, get back in the wagons, now!"

Tanuki readily complied, grabbing Gullin by the trouser leg and pulled him along to the harbor beneath Yofune's underside. David gouged the mirror with his arrowhead again, but Yofune snatched him away and stuck him down beneath his bristly chest. The gypsies had not understood Yofune, but David screamed the orders to them in English. They immediately sprinted back into the safety of the wagons. Once everyone was inside, Yofune coiled his serpentine body and tail around the wagons in a firm squeeze. He dug his claws into the ground as deeply as he could, and then hunkered down.

"Yofune, what is—" David's question was interrupted by the piercing whistle of wind, sneaking in from around the edges of the mirror.

"She is using an old Egyptian summons," Yofune said, his voice shaky with concern. "I recognize it. One of the dragon clans is from the western deserts, and I heard them speak of this summons a long time ago."

"What is this summons supposed to do?" David was shouting now, for the howling of wind was getting louder. Acacia raised her voice, chanting her spell at high volume.

"She is calling on a southern wind," Yofune shouted back, "One of the most powerful. It is the wind that shapes deserts and destroys seas. It is the wind that gave her clan protection when they were exiled in Egypt."

As David looked up towards the mirror, he watched as the small crack he had gouged grew bigger, until the wall was a spider's web of fissures. The mirror shattered into millions of shards as a violent desert wind roared down into the tunnel. Its strength threatened to knock Yofune off his feet and blow away the wagons. But the dragon remained fused to the earth, his mighty coils hanging on to the caravan. He lowered his head against the hurricane of scorching sand that barreled down on them.

The wind screeched and poured in around Acacia,

who remained transfixed as she chanted her summons. Part of her combined with the wind, as the feathers on her wings shed a black sand that whirled and whipped about like ghosts. The Will O' Wisps shrieked as the wind and sand smothered them out like candlelight. The smoke from their extinguishment was swallowed by the summoned cyclone. Not until every trace of fire was demolished did the sandstorm fade, and all was eerily quiet.

David lifted his head and opened his eyes to find himself half-buried in sand. Every inch of the tunnel's floor was blanketed in sand, and sunlight poured in from the mouth of the tunnel, only a few meters above them.

Yofune lifted his feet out of the sand, carefully loosening his coils from the wagons. Gullin and Tanuki crawled out from under him, sputtering and coughing.

"Dear Saint Bridget," Gullin hacked, uneasily standing up on the slippery sand. "This is why I hate magic."

David stood up, shaking the sand from his clothes. "At least we're safe and we can get out of here now, thanks to—"

He turned and saw Acacia lying face down in the sand. Her wings were in tatters, patches of skin visible through the weather-beaten feathers.

She was as still as death.

CHAPTER FIVE

Yofune Nushi once lived in a lair beneath the waters off the shores of Japan, before he renounced his old life of terrorizing humans for a new life of tranquil solitude on land. His old home was situated next to a tear in the Curtain, in a grotto carved from the face of a cliff overlooking the ocean. Once he and Tanuki got the caravan out of the swamp and back to Japan, Yofune escorted everyone to his old lair. The cave was invisible to anyone on land, and there was plenty of evidence—smashed boats, torn sails, and strewn debris—to show what happened to foolish sailors who attempted to sail in the lair's perilous reef. It was a home befitting a reclusive dragon of the seas.

The grotto led into a series of spacious chambers, rooms which were dry and warm. This was once a place where other sea dragons could come for gatherings or reunions, with all the trappings of sunken boats, valuable tributes, and treasures from the deepest depths of the ocean.

Yofune and Tanuki were relieved to be unburdened once they pulled the wagons with their passengers into the safety of the grotto. The gypsies filed out of the wagons, but Gullin and David stayed inside one of them with Acacia. They feared to move her, as she shivered violently when they tried to pick her up. From his bedchamber, Yofune brought them a massive cushion, a housewarming gift from a Chinese ti-lung, and they managed to lay Acacia onto it without much difficulty. The sickly bluish-green of the Shade was thick in her veins, so much that her pale skin was now tinted the faintest blue, and her tangled hair was a dull, chalky gray. Her paws, normally broad and strong, were withered into the spindly shape of crow's feet, and her wings were shedding feathers at a frightening rate. She resembled a sick kitten curled up on a pillow. Except for the shivering, she appeared comatose.

What was worse, where before Acacia had regained her color and strength after a short while of being stricken by the Shade, there had been no sign of improvement for over an hour.

"Why isn't she getting better?" Hot pinpricks of panic were rippling over David's skin. "Was it the summons? She's spoken spells before, but she got better later. Why did this happen?"

Yofune was in his human shape so he fit inside the wagon, and he sat down next to David. "The summons she called upon was very powerful. Such magic would have been taxing on anyone who was in perfect health, let alone her condition. She sacrificed a good deal of her strength, leaving little to fight against the Shade. I'm afraid it has overtaken her. She cannot hold it off on her own any longer."

"I don't like you two talking when I can't understand a blasted thing you're saying," Gullin grumbled at David and Yofune's conversing in Japanese. He leaned back in a chair, puffing irritably on his pipe.

Yofune turned his eye on Gullin. "It would benefit you to listen more closely, Huntsman, if you wish to understand. Language is a small matter if you can hear the words with your heart."

Gullin's face flushed. "So you do know English."

The blind man smirked. "I have had to deal with many dragon clans over the centuries, many of which hail from your part of the world. While we prefer our dragon tongue, it helps to be linguistically diverse, so we can identify the different threats humans pose to us."

"Smart of you." Gullin stood up, crossing his arms. "And you probably thought it a clever trick, pretending to be blind. But you cannot be, otherwise you could not know that I am a Huntsman without seeing my crest."

Yofune stroked his long beard. "You smell of blood, sweat, and metal. All the stenches of one who kills, but you do not have the evil stink of a murderer. You hunt for survival." The scarred eyes narrowed. "Although I venture to believe you have, perhaps once or twice, attempted to slay one of my brethren."

The Huntsman wrinkled his nose. "You're one to

accuse. You did not seem dismayed about your 'brethren' when your bloody badger blew him open—"

"Can we not argue about this?" David cut in. "We need to help Acacia. We have to get the Shade out of her."

Gullin faced David. "So she told you, then? I figured she would have." He knelt down next to the cushion, his hand touching Acacia's paw.

"No, I found out from—" David paused. "You knew about the Shade too?"

"Curse that demon Nyx," Gullin seethed. "I'd like to meet the witch myself, give her what's for." His fingers clasped Acacia's claws, his thumb rubbing the back of her paw.

"Did Acacia ever tell you if there was a way to remove it?"

Gullin shook his head. "I've tried every herb, medicine and antidote I know. This Shade isn't just a disease or poison. It's a parasite, buried so deep that there's no way to reach it."

"It is not the work of a hunter to cure," Yofune said. "It is the work for a healer."

"I do more than just kill, old man," Gullin muttered.

"Do you know of a healer who could help?" David asked, hoping to stop another argument before it began.

Yofune thought on this. "You wish to find someone whose abilities exceed the powers of a primordial goddess. There are few left who know the ways of the old gods, but even if one knew the secrets of Nyx, I fear no one would dare to oppose her will. It is her essence that flows in Acacia's veins."

"So you're telling me there's nothing we can do?" Gullin rose up and paced the room, his hands clasped behind his back. "There has to be something. Someone must know the nature of these ... these Shades."

David's brain weighed all the information he had, calculating at a spitfire speed. He jumped up. "Yofune, I need you to open a dream path to me. I know who can help us."

Even after having been to the world of sleep once before, it was no easier to navigate than it was the last time. David adjusted himself to the rosy-hued dream atmosphere, recognizing the assemblage of dreamers, dreams, and emotions around him.

He did not have time to enjoy it. Immediately, he called out with his thoughts. *Hypnos, I must speak with you! I'm David Sandoval. I was the one looking for the sphinx. Are you here?*

I am here.

The hazy shape of Hypnos appeared before him, creating a ripple of blue in the crimson-tinted environment.

David's thoughts rambled out incoherently, as human minds do when under stress. *Hypnos, my friend is dying.*

Your mother's Shade is killing her. You must know how these Shades work. You must help me get rid of it. What can I do? Is there a healer who can banish it? Is there some magic that can combat it? Can you remove it? Please, I need help! You must help me!

Hypnos held up a hand, and David's mind instantly quieted. The warden of Sleep showed no sign of compassion or sympathy, his voice void of emotion. ***Why must I help you? It is no business of mine. I do not meddle in my mother's affairs.***

But Acacia will die!

As we all do, someday.

She is in pain!

Life is pain.

David felt himself glowing red, turning into pure heat. His thoughts became jumbled again. *Why do you allow this? Why do you allow Nyx to destroy others for her own selfish desires? Why is she doing this? What does she need Acacia's cleverness for? If she's a goddess, she should have everything she wants already. Does no one care? Does no one care that Nyx is ripping people apart for no reason? Do you not care about anyone but yourself?*

Hypnos raised his hand again, cutting off David's thoughts. ***Do not question whether I sympathize or not. My role is to care for the dreamers in my world. But, if you must know, I do not agree with my mother's desires. And your sphinx is a more beautiful dreamer than most. Her suffering did touch me. I was moved to give her gifts*** *that I have given only the rarest of dreamers, to ease her pain. But I cannot remove the Shade from her.*

David's anger cooled. *You gave her gifts?*

She cannot speak aloud without feeling pain, so I gave her the gift to speak to others in their dreams. She may calm the minds of men and women with her breath, and bestow the most comforting sleep with her gaze. These gifts allow her to protect herself when she becomes too weak to fight. On her own, she found a way of glimpsing others' memories and personal thoughts through their dreams. An invasive hobby, but sphinxes are enthralled by the workings of the mind.

David could not believe he had not wondered where Acacia had gotten her abilities. His mission, however, did not give him time to appreciate Hypnos's generosity. *But Acacia can't defend herself anymore. The Shade's made her too weak. Even when she tried to tell me something important, she could barely get a few words out without—*

What was she trying to tell you? Hypnos seemed to smile, but it was hard to tell since his features were blurred.

She was telling me ... David's thoughts were muddled momentarily, until Hypnos helped isolate his random memories. *Acacia was trying to tell me about a vision she had. She said someone told her she had to find someone, and she thought it might have been me.*

Hypnos did not say anything. He emanated a pulse that made David feel he was on the right track.

Do you know what she was trying to tell me? David asked.

I do. She was told an oracle by a priestess many years ago. She has dreamt about it often, Hypnos replied.

David was filled with both curiosity and dread. *What was it? Can you tell me? Does it have to do with me? Does it have to do with the Shade?*

Oracles tend to be cryptic, Hypnos replied. **But perhaps, a boy as intelligent as you can help give it meaning.**

Hypnos dissolved back into the dream atmosphere, and David found the rosy mist swirling into a yellow-gold ambiance. There were vague shapes of the sun, and a brown plain dotted with strange golden triangles. It took him a minute, but David recognized that the triangles symbolized pyramids. A long blue streak cut through the plain—a river. The scenery had the soft gauzy appearance of a watercolor painting. David wondered if this was how Acacia saw the world, for he guessed that Hypnos was recreating the vision that she had about her oracle.

A female voice of maturity and wisdom spoke to him:

To vanquish the Shade's poison aura
You must use guidance from three flora
The one you seek bears the scent of the lily white.
When he first sees you, he will show no fright.
A golden flower you will not touch or see

Is a promise he will give to strengthen thee.
The violet plucked will release his special voice
And with its power, awaken the Singing Turquoise.
The Shade shall be imprisoned forever in stone …

The voice faded away, and the yellow glow of the dream morphed into a vibrant green field, with a solid blue sky. The triangles changed into a tan color with smoke seeping out the tops of them. This image endured for as long as the blink of an eye before it all dissipated back into the scarlet mist of Hypnos' world.

Wait! Was that it? David inquired. *The person who can get rid of the Shade bears lilies? He'll make a promise, and something about picking a violet … and there's something made of turquoise …* He focused his mind, and repeated the oracle slowly, until it was cemented in his memory. He found that it was easier to remember things without the limits of the physical body affecting his short term memory.

The one you seek bears a white lily … a white lily! David remembered where he had seen one of those.

While it was good that he deduced the meaning of the first clue, he felt a pang of despondency. *It isn't me,* he thought. *I'm not the one who can save Acacia. But I know who is.*

David blinked his eyes open as he returned from the sleep realm. He was sitting next to a bonfire. The gypsies were huddled around him, watching with intrigue. Yofune stood behind him, waiting patiently. David stood up, regained the feeling in his legs, and he beckoned Yofune to join him inside the wagon. Inside, Gullin was watching over Acacia, who showed no sign of improvement. Tanuki, tuckered out from the events of the day, was curled up on the edge of the pillow by Acacia's feet.

"Hypnos told me that Acacia was given an oracle that tells how to save her," he told them, and he recited the oracle.

Gullin huffed. "Why can't oracles say anything outright? Just fortune-teller nonsense."

"It at least gives us an idea where to start," David said.

"Start? Start where?" Gullin's expression hardened. "Are we supposed to go flower picking? You didn't say anything about a place, or a cure, or anything that is remotely helpful! And what nonsense is this Singing Turquoise? It's a color! How do you make a color sing?"

"I figured out that part with the lily," David said. "It should be obvious to you, Gullin. You've been carrying one around with you for a long time."

Gullin looked down at the tattoo on his arm. "You mean my crest? Would make sense, wouldn't it?" The frown on his face implied that he wasn't in agreement. "But 'the golden flower you will not touch or see'? What's that, oh brilliant one?"

177

David frowned at the mockery. "I assume it's a metaphor. It's a promise that can strengthen Acacia, maybe some kind of magic incantation that can weaken the Shade. I haven't figured out the part after that, about the violet and the special voice." He ran his fingers through his hair. "Violet is a girl's name, so maybe it means we need to find a woman who sings? Maybe one of the sirens ... but none of them were named Violet or had feathers of that color. It could be someone who grows violets, or wears something violet."

"Mibbae it means one of us sings like a girl," Gullin offered, shifting his eyes in David's direction.

David rested his chin on his hand, thinking. "There must be a connection between the colors. White, gold, violet, turquoise. I don't know. Do you know what any of the clues might mean, Master Yofune?"

The sage sat quietly for a minute, breathing very deeply as he thought. "The Shade of Nyx would be imprisoned in stone, after the Singing Turquoise is awakened. That is what you said?"

David nodded.

"Perhaps turquoise does not mean the color. It means the stone. A Singing Stone." He rested his eyelids, and a tired smile set in his lips. "I have heard of the Singing Stones before. There was a dragon of distant kindred, the Piasa, who spoke of the Singing Stones in his homeland. From what I understand, the humans who live there believe that certain stones hold mystical powers to heal or harm. The Singing Stones were gifts from a spirit of the earth, bestowed to the shamans of several tribes, to be shared among the various clans. When the stones were used properly, they would break their silence and fill the earth with song. They brought fertility to the harvest and prosperity to the people. But humans' greed led to jealousy, and each tribe wanted to collect all the Singing Stones for themselves. Many wars were fought for the stones, so the spirit took them back to hide them from man. Only humans who prove themselves true and honorable can sway the earth spirit to grant them the gift of a Singing Stone."

"An earth spirit ..." David felt a surge of hope. The earth spirit could be the one the vision was talking about. If it was the keeper of the Singing Stones, one of them could be a turquoise. If anything, an earth spirit might have the knowledge to clarify what the oracle could mean.

"What is the place this dragon was from? What is the Piasa's homeland?" he asked.

"The faraway plains in the land across the great ocean. You would know it as America in the North," Yofune answered.

"America?" Gullin let out a long whistle. "You want us to go trampin' around in that backwards country full of pompous eejits? Still, can't help but like the lot a little, for showin' it to the bloody English."

David remembered the image of the green plain and blue sky that he had seen in Acacia's vision. A faraway plain across the ocean—but there were lots of green plains with clear blue skies all over the world. Yet something told him that it could not be coincidence that the vision matched what Yofune had described. A Singing Turquoise could be hidden in the American plains. It felt right.

"I think we should go find this earth spirit," David said, "and find out if the Singing Turquoise is one of the stones it guards."

"Oh, that's a piece of pie," Gullin scoffed. "Let's just start at one end of America, and walk all the way to the other end, and surely we'll just stumble into this earth spirit. Or maybe we'll just stand on the highest mountain and call out for it like a couple of ravin' loons. Even if we could find it, what do we do, invite it over for crumpets and ask it if it'll just hand over its rocks? Take it from me, flesh-and-blood beasts are hard enough to track. Spirits are impossible, boyo."

"Should we just sit here and do nothing?" David argued. "There has to be a way to figure out where in America we could find this spirit. If the Piasa knows of it, the spirit might live in the same region as he does. We could go talk to him and ask."

"That would not be wise," Yofune warned. "The Piasa is a man-eater, and unlike myself, he has not renounced his flesh-devouring ways. He is also fiercely territorial. Even I, a fellow dragon, would be given no hospitality from him in his homeland."

David tapped his fingers together as he pondered. "Master Yofune, when Hypnos was showing me Acacia's vision, there was a grassy meadow that had triangle-shaped houses on it, with smoke coming from the tops. Did the Piasa ever speak of people in America who live in houses like that? It might be a specific town, and maybe that's where we need to go."

"Indians," Gullin said dryly.

Both David and Yofune gawked at him.

"Those were houses of Indian nomads." Gullin grinned, liking that he knew something that David did not. "One of my brothers went over to America years ago, to try his luck digging for gold like most of the loonies out there. He sent letters and photographs back home while he was traveling to the west. He came across Indians living in tents made of the skins of large animals they call bison. Said they tend to keep to themselves mostly, but they don't get along too well with the locals."

David knew what bison were from a book he had read about adventurers' exploits to the New World. Bison were bigger than bulls, and shaggy like sheep. He had also read about the American Indians, people with tanned skin who wore feathers and animal skins for clothes, and lived on the wide open plains. They were just as mysterious and fantastic as any of the mythological tales he loved. He was not sure where in America the bison and native plainsmen dwelled, or if America was the place that the oracle had been indicating. But they were short of time, and Gullin's description was close to matching the vision. "This is good. The Indians may know about the Singing Stones or the earth spirit. We want to go to wherever there are wide open plains with lots of bison. Let's go through the Curtain to get there."

Gullin scratched his chin. "I hear bison country's an awfully big place. We could be wandering around there for miles and miles and not find anything. Who's to say the Curtain would lead us straight to this earth spirit we're looking for?"

"Spirits are not confined by the limits of the flesh as we are," Yofune noted. "Being an essence of the earth, it is possible that it can be called upon anywhere on its sacred land, as long as it is a pure place untainted by the industry of man."

David stood up from the floor, dusting off his trousers. "We won't know unless we go there. Yofune, can you take me through the Curtain to America?"

The sage let out a long exhale. "Sandoval-san, it is a very far distance to go, even through the Curtain. My exertions from fighting the Sleepless Dragon and escaping the fox-man's den have made me tired. You must give me time to rest."

"But look at Acacia! We don't have time to rest! I can't go all by myself—"

"Of course you're not going by yourself!" Gullin barked. "You're hunting for this earth spirit. I'm a Master Huntsman. I've been trained since I was a younger pup than you for tracking down the untraceable. Besides, the oracle says I have a hand in all this, right?" He tapped the lily on his tattoo.

David had mixed feelings about it. As much as he and Gullin had gotten to know each other, he was uneasy about being in a strange land alone with the Huntsman. He wondered if Gullin would treat him differently if Acacia was not around. David had to admit, however, that Gullin had more hunting experience than he did. Given how devoted the Scotsman was to the sphinx, he would put all of his effort into finding the Singing Turquoise as much as David would.

"You're right. You need to come." David placed his hand on Gullin's shoulder in a gesture of friendship.

Gullin sneered at David's hand. "You ever work a day in your life, lad? You got soft baby-bottom hands."

David withdrew his hand. Gullin smirked.

"I will stay and watch over the others," Yofune said. "The fox-man and his allies should not be able to find my home, but I will not leave your clan unguarded. I will have Tanuki guide you through the Curtain."

"Does he know his way through the Curtain by himself?" David asked.

Yofune leaned over and nudged the snoring badger. Tanuki snorted awake, blinking his eyes. "Is it time for supper already?" he asked with a yawn.

The blind man chuckled softly. "Tanuki my friend, I need you to guide David-san and the hunter on a quest to help the sphinx. You must take them through the Curtain to the America in the North."

"Oh, okay. Right after I have my pre-dinner sake." Tanuki stretched, and scratched his right ear. It took him a moment to comprehend what Yofune had requested, and when he did, his fur bristled on end. "Wait, I have to take them where? By myself? Oh, no no no, Master. I've never gone through the Curtain without you, and I've never been to that land. I'll get terribly lost—"

"You'll be fine. You have been my eyes for a long time, and your sense of smell is as acute as mine. Trust the folds of the Curtain to guide you in the right direction."

The badger darted his eyes back and forth. "Is this going to be dangerous? I've had enough danger for one day. And if it's got anything to do with that crazy goddess you were talking about, forget it."

Yofune frowned, but spoke with patience. "It is a searching quest. David and the hunter need to find a special stone. They know who they need to ask for it. They just need you to help them get to where they need to go."

"But … but … the red-headed man …" Tanuki lowered his voice, even though Gullin could not translate his Japanese. "He scares me. And he smells funny."

"Then just focus on David-san. He doesn't scare you, and he doesn't smell."

Tanuki huffed in defeat. He knew better than to argue with his master. He stood up, cracking his back with a final stretch. "All right. But I'm taking them there, and that's all. I'm not getting involved with any more hazards to my health. And I'm not responsible for what happens to them."

David patted Tanuki's head. "Thank you, Tanuki."

The badger looked up at him, twitching his whiskers. "You're welcome. After all, what would you do without the most divine creature in Japan?"

"You've moved up from the most divine in Kyoto to all of Japan?"

Tanuki stuck out his chest in pride. "Now that I'm going over to America to share my splendor, I may be the most divine creature in the world!"

"Would you two shut your jabbering gobs already?" Gullin snapped. "If you're done blabbering, we've got us a Singing Stone to find."

CHAPTER TWELVE

Tanuki had chosen the form of an elk so he could run swiftly, while David and Gullin rode on his back. America, however, proved to be trickier to find than one might think. Tanuki bounded through the smoky fog between the supernatural realm and the human-ruled world for what seemed like hours. Eventually they crossed over into a dusty, dry land with tall trees bearing feathery fronds at the tops—they reminded David of feather dusters. There was a watering hole, where an extraordinarily huge animal was bathing. It had gray wrinkled skin, large tree-trunk legs, and it sprayed water on its back with its long hose of a nose.

"See? I told you I'd get you here. That must be a bison right there," Tanuki said.

David shook his head. "I've seen pictures of that animal before. It's not a bison. It's an elephant. They live in Africa and India."

Tanuki tilted his head. "You told me you needed to go to the place where Indians live. Wouldn't Indians live in India?"

"Yes … I mean, no … the Indians we want to find are different. Not *India* Indians, American Indians."

The shape-shifter sighed in exasperation. "You need to tell me these things! I'm divine, but not psychic."

Back through the Curtain, Tanuki continued his search. He tried to pick up hints and scents from the pockets of the misty veil around him. Their trek evolved into a site-seeing tour, as they briefly caught glimpses of Austria ("It sounds like America," Tanuki retorted), Australia ("It sounds like Austria … wait, which country are we looking for?"), Morocco ("What? It smelled yummy!"), and Brazil ("What do you mean, SOUTH America? There are two?").

Finally, as Tanuki was about to call it quits and go home to Japan, the group fell out of the Curtain and landed with a heavy thump on soft ground. David landed square on his back, and was knocked breathless. When he opened his eyes, he was staring up at a blue sky, bordered by long swaying strands of meadow grass. Somewhere not far off, he heard the sound of a rushing river.

A large black snout hovered over his face, sniffing his hair.

David's eyes bulged, and he cautiously scooted away so he could sit up. Once he did, he became mesmerized by the complacent face of the animal, a bison. The bison regarded him calmly, and lowered its massive muzzle to the ground to munch on the prairie grass.

Gullin was already standing up and marveling at the bison. He ventured to place a hand on its shoulder, petting the furry hide. "You're a big girl. But you're a gentle giant, aren't you? Wonder if the locals around here tame these beasts."

David stood up, rubbing the back of his aching legs. He glanced around at the wide expanse of terrain. They were in a pasture embellished with hills that popped up like half-formed bubbles on the surface of water. The grass was tall enough to reach their knees, and it was dotted with wildflowers. "Speaking of locals, there doesn't seem to be a town around here. Maybe we should scout around. Too bad we can't ask the bison for directions."

Tanuki shifted back into badger shape. "Allow me. We animals share common languages." He approached the bison, and spoke in a chattering language. The bison kept chewing the grass, seemingly ignoring the badger.

"Hmm, obviously this cow is behind the times," Tanuki sighed. "Maybe I should try something more primitive." He tried again, in a more guttural tongue. He spoke in a series of different tones, to which the bison stared at him with its blank black eyes.

Gullin sat down on a rock a few paces off, and cracked his neck. "We might as well get comfortable. I bet the gopher's going to take a while to get anything out of that one."

David sat down on the ground, pondering whether

he should go off and look around. Tanuki, meanwhile, grew increasingly frustrated with the bison, but out of sheer determination kept trying to find a common dialect. Fifteen minutes later, Tanuki returned to his companions. "That cow talks really funny, but I think I figured out what she was saying. She didn't say we were in America. She says her family has always called this place the Land where the Herd Will Live Forever. I think that's what she said. It was more like, 'Laaaaaaaaaaaand wheeeeeeeere the Heeeeeeeeeeeeeerd Wiiiiiill Liiiiiiiiiiiiive Foooooooooooooreeeeeeeeeeeeveee eeeeeeeeeer."

"The herd? There are more bison nearby?" David asked, growing excited. "Tanuki, can you go ask the bison if she or any of the herd knows about an earth spirit, or the Singing Stones?"

Tanuki snorted, his ears twitching. "What would you do without me, David-san?" He waddled back over to the bison, who continued munching her leafy lunch.

Gullin rested his elbows on his knees, musing over the bison. "That old girl reminds me of the sheep we used to herd back home. Not quite as big as this Bessie, of course." He cast his gaze over at David. "Why are you doing all of this, David?"

"What do you mean?"

"Jumping halfway around the world, looking for a spirit that could very well doom you to the netherworld as anything, searching for a stone that may or may not be the answer to this vision you were told about. That's an awful lot of trouble to go through, and you're not even sure if you're right."

"I feel in my gut that this is what we need to do."

Gullin laughed, shaking his head. "You feel it in your gut. Spoken like a true greenhorn. Let's say your 'gut' is right. What do you get out of this?"

David paused, trying to figure out what it was that Gullin was implying. "I'm not doing this for me. Acacia is dying. I don't know if the Singing Turquoise is here or not, or if it will save her, but we don't have clues to anything else."

Gullin's eyes darkened. "You don't expect me to believe you're doing this solely for her, do you? If you're just doing this to get back home, I can send you back home. It's no loss to me. But if you're aiming to get something out of her, I'll—"

"What is the matter with you?" David had enough of this distrust out of Gullin. "I know you want to help Acacia too, so why do you care about my reason—"

"Don't call her that." Gullin's voice was ominous, although it was little more than a whisper.

David was debating whether to prod further to find out what had triggered Gullin's sudden mood change, when Tanuki tugged on the cuff of his trousers.

"She said she doesn't know anything about any stones," Tanuki reported. "She doesn't know what a spirit is, either. She said something about the Great Mother of the Herd that Protects Us, but she called me dumb for not knowing what that was, so I'm not talking to her anymore." He crossed his little arms and raised his nose into the air.

Gullin smirked. "I don't suppose you speak Bison too, boyo?" he asked.

David's shoulders slumped, and he stuck his hands in his pockets. "Let's look around. Maybe we'll spot a town nearby."

No sooner did they begin to walk away, Gullin clutched David by the arm and yanked him down into the tall grass.

"Ow! Gullin, what—" David's voice was loud with indignation, but Gullin slapped a hand over his mouth.

"Quiet, we've got company," Gullin whispered.

Peeking cautiously over the top of the grass, they watched as a dark shape moved across the plain, hunkered low to the earth. It appeared to be a smaller bison, for it had the same dark brown fur and horns. However, the skin hung too loosely, and it slinked by smoothly, not with a heavy animal's lumbering gate. To add to the confusion, the smaller bison emitted a deep bellow that did not sound natural. It caught the attention of the female bison, who lifted her great head and turned towards it.

"What is that?" David whispered. "Something is off about that bison."

"Because it's not a bison," Gullin muttered, and he

cracked his knuckles. "It's clear as day that noise is a calling horn. It's a hunter."

"A hunter, like you?"

Gullin shook his head. "We Master Huntsmen have a strict law in our guild not to kill a fellow human, unless in self defense. This hunter might not follow the same law."

"Then let's wait until he moves on," David suggested. He did not doubt Gullin could scare off an opposing hunter, but they couldn't see if the bison-skinned man had any weapons. Since the only weapon Gullin had was Orthros, it was too perilous to confront the stranger. He could have a bow and arrows, or a musket.

Gullin shook his head. "He's already spotted us, boyo. I doubt he's alone. It would take more than one man to bring down a beast that big."

He had a point, and given that the grass was tall, more men could be hiding anywhere around them. The bison-skinned man called with the horn again, this time in two long howls and then one short blow—David worried that it was a warning to other hunters that may be nearby. The female bison started plodding towards the horn's call.

Then they heard the rumbling.

From around the base of a hill came a stampeding herd of bison, as many as fifty or sixty. A brigade of warrior natives on horseback pursued them, hollering up a storm to keep the herd running. The mass of hooves, muscles and horns was heading straight towards the two men and the badger. The three scrambled to stand up and bolted as if the Mouth of the Underworld was closing in to swallow them up.

As David ran, he had a split second to be in awe of the natives' cunning hunting tactics. The one native with the calling horn must have summoned enough of the bison from the nearby area to be within range, and then the remaining hunters funneled the herd towards a spot where there was probably a trap set and ready to snare several bison. He would have loved to make notes of this in his journal, if he wasn't in danger of being trampled to death.

The female bison joined the panic and barreled ahead, lowing with urgency. Tanuki scurried to keep up with David and Gulluin, but tripped and tumbled head over paws. He was lost among the massive bison as they trampled the ground around him.

David stopped and turned around. His friend disappeared in the kicked-up dust and the tumult of rampaging giants. "Tanuki!"

"Don't be daft!" Gullin called back as he kept running. Suddenly, he halted and came dashing back to David, his face tightened into a vicious snarl. David froze, thinking that Gullin had figured out an opportunity to get rid of him by knocking him into the oncoming bison. He was about to take his chances and escape back through the herd, when he saw the actual reason Gullin was running back to him. One of the hunters had spotted David, and his horse was galloping in pursuit towards him. In one fluid movement, the hunter swooped his arm down, nabbed David by the back of his shirt, and hoisted him belly-down onto his saddle. Gullin caught up to the horse and grabbed the hunter by the leg, wrenching him off his saddle and throwing him down on the ground. If there had been a moment to spare, David would have pointed out the contrariness of Gullin calling him "daft" while he was tackling an armed warrior barehanded.

David was thrown from the horse, and hit the ground heavily. His heart raced as he saw the nearing bulk of a bison that was sure to crush him. In half a second, he was yanked out of the bison's path, clobbered on the back of the head, and sent into unconscious oblivion.

When David came to, there were no more bison. But there were many tan angry faces looking down at him, with stone-headed arrows pointing at his body.

Gullin had faired no better. He sat next to David, his hands tied behind his back with leather straps. "How's your brain there, boyo? Not too broken, I hope."

David tried to sit up slowly, but he too was bound. He regarded his captors, and he spoke slowly. "We don't mean you harm. We're friends. We need your help."

"They tie us up, with arrows in our faces, and you're telling them *we* don't mean any harm? You must've been hit hard." Gullin shook his head. "It's no good anyway. They don't speak our language, or at least don't want to."

The expressions on the natives' faces did not lose their tense, suspicious glare. One of the warriors said something to them, but it was in his indigenous language, and neither Gullin nor David understood. But the command was threatening enough that neither of them moved or replied. The natives searched the two of them over, confiscating Gullin's Orthros, David's dagger, and his pouch of herb pellets. They also found his makeshift cross in his pocket, which caused the men to speak quickly to each other. David wondered why that item, of all things, made them react that way. He and Gullin were forced onto their feet, and the natives walked them over to where five horses were left grazing in a field. They were loaded onto one of the horses and carried off for what they predicted would be an unpleasant ride.

David was seated back-to-back with Gullin, facing the rear of the horse and looking out at the landscape behind them. He spotted a rabbit tailing after them with determined swiftness. The rabbit, with its familiar fur coloring and a blackish-brown scruff of tail rather than a white puff, was only a slight distortion of his true badger form, and David was somewhat relieved to know their friend had not abandoned them.

Somewhat. He would have been more relieved to know what exactly was in store for them.

CHAPTER THIRTEEN

The Native American settlement was a scattering of the nomadic tents that Gullin had talked about before, and seeing them only heightened David's hopes, for they were surely the same shapes he had seen in Acacia's dream. The people of the tribe tended to small gardens of food-bearing plants, tanned animal skins, and went about their daily tasks in much the same way David and his family completed chores. The thought of it made him miss home very much. He even found himself longing for Acacia's adoptive family and their brightly colored caravan.

The tribespeople stopped what they were doing when they saw David and Gullin being carried in. A curious silence hung in the air as the Scotsman and boy were pulled down off the horse, hands still bound, and led to one of the tribe's largest tents.

Inside, the tent was adorned with various talismans and ritualistic relics that David had never seen before in any book. A small fire burned in a pit. Across the fire sat what could presumably be the oldest relic in the room, a silver-haired man with trenches of wrinkles in his skin, his frail body covered in a cloak made from the bronze-brown fur of a bear. He appeared asleep at first, for his head was lowered and he made no movement. When one of the hunters spoke to the elder in their native tongue, the ancient one lifted his head and looked at them with wizened, dark eyes.

"Please, sir, we didn't mean to—" David was instantly cut off from saying more, as the warrior holding him smacked him on the back of the head.

The shaman reprimanded the young hunter in a rasping but authoritative tone. He regarded David for several moments of silence. "You are strangers here."

David let out a sigh of relief that this shaman could speak English. "Yes, we come from very far away. We didn't mean to trespass on your land. We are not a threat to you."

One of the hunters brought the shaman the items that they had taken from David and Gullin. The shaman looked over the items, and picked up David's cross. "Have you come to teach us about your God, like the others who have come here bearing this symbol?"

David's jaw dropped open, and he stuttered for a moment. "N-no, no, that's … I'm here on a mission. My friend is dying, which no medicine can cure. I need your help."

The shaman nodded. "I see. If there is no medicine to cure your friend, then what is it that you seek?"

"We were told there might be something called a …"

David paused, glancing back at Gullin. The Huntsman tilted his head in the shaman's direction, as a sign for David to continue. The young man swallowed before he spoke again. "Do you know of the Singing Stones?"

Everyone in the tent was quiet for a long time. The shaman narrowed his eyes, rubbing his chin as he scrutinized the boy from head to toe. The hunters looked back and forth between each other, and some of them put their hands on the knives tucked into their belts.

Eventually the shaman rested his hands in his lap. "Where have you heard of this?"

"I saw it in a dream," David answered, but he thought that explanation sounded childish. "I mean, I was shown a vision …" He stopped, thinking this sounded even more ridiculous, but the shaman's eyebrows lifted.

"Ah, a vision." A smile crept into the multitude of wrinkle lines of the shaman's face. "Visions can be very important. But what you may believe is a vision could be a trick. Perhaps it was just a dream."

"No, this was real. This isn't a trick," David insisted. "I wouldn't have come all this way if I didn't believe it was true."

The shaman contemplated David's earnest reply. He spoke to the hunters, and they cut off the bindings around David and Gullin's wrists. The hunters left except for one, who remained at the opening of the tent, his eyes locked on the two strangers.

"Sit," the shaman invited, and David and Gullin

complied. "Perhaps you have been guided here by the great spirits. Or you may have been taught to be spies to gain our trust. But there would be very few who could have told you about the stones. Where do you come from?"

David made an uncomfortable laugh. "To be honest, sir, I have been so many places in the last few days, I'm not sure how to answer your question."

The shaman turned to Gullin. "Are you this boy's guardian?"

Gullin smirked. "Only by circumstance."

"How did you come to our land?"

David and Gullin both hesitated, wondering if the shaman would actually believe the truth. If he didn't believe them, would he ask the hunter behind them to dispatch them? Finally, David replied, "We were guided here through the Curtain by a badger."

Gullin stifled a laugh at David's oversimplified answer.

"The Curtain?" the shaman asked.

"It's …" David pursed his lips as he tried to think of how to explain. "It's the pathway between this world and …another one. Or several other ones, I don't know."

The shaman was intrigued. "You were led here from the spirit world by a guide in the form of a badger?"

David blurted out, "Yes, exactly," before he even knew what he was saying.

The shaman nodded slowly. "We of the Lakota believe that every man is born with a spirit guide. You were led here by the badger, the animal of courage and healing. I believe you are telling the truth about your quest. However, no one may find the Singing Stones. They have been lost to man for a long time."

David felt his heart sink, but he wouldn't be defeated that easily. "I was told the stones belong to an earth spirit. Do you know about this spirit?"

"There are many spirits of the earth," the shaman replied. "They live in the soil, the grass, the food we grow. They protect the balance of all things, and protect both man and animal. Yet if the Great Mystery believes it best for man to be kept from the Stones, then that is its will, not ours."

"The Great Mystery?" David remembered a similar term he had recently heard. "Is that like The Great Mother that Protects Us?"

The shaman was quiet again for a moment. "Was this also in your vision?"

"No, a bison told us." David caught himself again. "I know that sounds silly, but—"

"You speak to the bison?" the shaman asked. A look of dawning realization passed over his face. "Ptesan-Wi."

"Te-san-what?" Gullin asked.

"Ptesan-Wi, the blessed White Calf. The one who passes between the bison and the people. Long ago, she taught the Lakota many of our tribe's rituals and bestowed on us the *chanunpa* so we may worship the Great Mystery." The shaman sighed with satisfaction.

"Your spirit guide has brought you here to seek Ptesan-Wi, so she may show you the way to heal your friend."

"Where can we find this Ptesan-Wi?" David asked, leaning forward.

The shaman frowned. "The White Calf is the most holy of all creatures. It is not a matter of finding her as one would hunt the deer or rabbit. You must be pure and strong of heart. Those who displease Ptesan-Wi will be destroyed by her."

Gullin mumbled under his breath, "In other words, like any woman."

"Do not insult the White Calf," the shaman warned. He turned back to David. "You must go out into the forest and have another vision. Let the badger spirit guide you. You must go without food or water or weapon. Once you have shed the trappings of the body, then you can see with your soul. Ptesan-Wi may reveal herself to you. If she does, you must not approach her. You must allow her to show you the path."

"How long might that take?" David asked.

"There is no telling. It could be many days."

"But I don't have that kind of time! My friend could be dead by then!"

The shaman's face was emotionless, although it was hard to tell past the layers of creases in his skin. "If it is the Great Mystery's will that your friend becomes one with all things, then there is no course of action you can take to prevent it." He turned his head towards Gullin.

"It is tradition that this journey be taken alone. You may stay here until your ward returns."

"Oh no, I don't think so," Gullin retorted. "This pup can't take three steps without something trying to kill him. My job is to make sure he comes back alive. Where he goes, I go."

The shaman sighed. "You may accompany him into the forest. When he receives the first signs of his vision, then he must go on alone."

Gullin frowned, but he nodded. He stood up, dusting off his trousers. "There's no time like the present. Let's go."

"One more thing before you go," the shaman interjected. He beckoned David to him with a welcoming wave of his hand. David went to him, kneeling down and bringing his ear close to the shaman's lips. "Remember to listen very closely to everything around you, and its meaning will become clear," he advised. "You may even discover the meaning of the flowers."

David looked into the shaman's eyes, stunned. The wise man grinned.

The Lakota hunters escorted David and Gullin out of the village and across the expanse of plain, until they came to the edge of the forest. There, the two companions dismounted their horses and walked off into the thick wood, only David glancing back over his shoulder at the Lakota who watched them go.

"You don't suppose they'll come after us, as part of a test?" David wondered.

"I doubt that they'd go through the trouble," Gullin replied. "There are plenty of things out here that can kill us as is. I'm sure they don't think we'll return."

David's breath grew rapid, as he took in the forest around him. It reminded him of his walk in the forest of Kyoto: tranquil but uneasy, as anything could be crouched in wait behind the foliage. He had read of bears, wolves, cougars, and other vicious American beasts. While all this should have seemed minute compared to creatures he had seen from the Curtain, he didn't have his dagger or Acacia to help him.

The two tramped along through the wilderness for hours in complete silence, save David's occasional attempts at starting a conversation that fell flat after a sentence or two. He was not sure how deep into the woods they were supposed to go, or if they walked all the way through, should they turn around and head back? Or were they meant to keep hiking until their feet fell off? Of course, they would probably starve before that would happen, or be eaten by something else.

He noticed that the daylight was rapidly fading, and a chill was settling down on them. "Maybe we should start looking for a place to set up camp," he suggested.

"Set up a camp with what?" Gullin asked.

David frowned. "All I'm saying is, if we see a good area where we wouldn't be too vulnerable to animal attack, we should spend the night there. But let's talk more about the oracle. Maybe we can figure it out a little better before we find Ptesan-Wi."

Gullin shrugged. "If we find her."

"Of course we will. We have to."

"You're a lad full of optimism, aren't you?" Gullin shoved his hands into his pockets. "Because this is like one of your la-de-da stories. You're the hero, and you'll get a happy ending. Heaven forbid you're wrong, and we don't find this Singing Turquoise. It has to be that easy for you, being the special one."

David snagged Gullin by the shoulder, tugging him to a halt. "That's enough. I understand, all right? When we find Ptesan-Wi, you ask for the stone. You have to be the one that saves Acacia. The oracle said as much." David's gaze dropped to the ground, and he kept walking.

Gullin walked behind him. "I've given your theory some thought. Why do you think that just because I have a tattoo of a lily on my arm, that the oracle was talking about me?"

"What else could it be talking about? '*The one you seek bears a lily white.*' It seems on the nose to me."

"Too on the nose, don't you think? And that's not what the oracle said."

"Yes it—" David paused, taking a moment to recall the vision. "*The one you seek bears ...*"

"The *scent* of the lily white. I don't exactly smell like a flower, boyo."

"Who does, then?"

It took Gullin several seconds to answer, as if he didn't want to tell what he was thinking. "There's a reason why the Master Huntsmen chose the white lily as a symbol in our crest. A lily stands for purity and innocence, to be borne by those pure of heart and soul. Acacia has her ways of knowing who's a good soul and who's not. I'm thinking, mibbae she can even smell such goodness in humans. She might be able to sniff out a boy who's pure of heart. A boy who smells so pure, he drew her to him while she was trying to return a pilfered purse."

David stopped dead in his tracks. He couldn't have been more floored than if he had been kicked by a horse. "That night at the inn! You think she was sniffing me, because she thinks I smell pure of heart? Am I the one the oracle was talking about? That could be what it meant! If Ptesan-Wi only reveals herself to those who are pure of heart, then she might show herself to me. I can save Acacia!"

His excitement was quickly quelled as Gullin's glare silenced him. The Huntsman turned away and kept on walking. David tried to think of something to say, but came up empty.

The two traveled on in silence for a while.

"Maybe it's not me," David said. "I mean, it's only a theory."

Gullin didn't reply.

"Leave it, then. We already know it's the Singing

Turquoise we need, and we'll get it. The oracle could've been about you, or me, and we're both here so either way one of us will find the stone."

No response.

David continued on. "So the second flower isn't a literal flower, from what I can tell. It's a promise, but then why does the oracle refer to it as a golden flower? Maybe it's a term that has a floral name. Like a 'forget-me-not.' It might mean a promise for someone not to forget something, or someone. Or it could mean a certain symbolism associated with flowers, like beauty or femininity. It could be a promise of something beautiful."

"You think too hard, boyo," Gullin mumbled.

David leapt easily over a tree root, and leaned against the tree. "If you have another theory you would like to offer, by all means, share it."

Gullin paused, looking over at the boy. "What is the most powerful promise someone can make, lad?"

David was surprised by the question. "Most powerful?"

"A promise so strong, so great, that it can give someone incredible strength, even to battle death?" Gullin crossed his arms, staring David down.

"I ... I'm not sure what you mean. A promise that can fight death?" He crinkled his face as he pondered. "A promise of ... immortality?"

Gullin slapped his hand to his forehead. "For the love of Pete! I'm asking the only hot-blooded young buck on earth who wouldn't know the answer to this. That's what comes from spending time with all those books, and no lasses."

David found Gullin's remark ridiculous. "I've spent plenty of time with 'lasses'! I don't see what that has to do with anything."

"Love, boyo! A promise of love!" Gullin was positively fuming, but David couldn't imagine why. "And you've already given one, without knowing it, of course." The Scotsman sat down on a fallen tree trunk, resting his hands on his knees.

"What are you ..." David's eyes widened. "You mean, to Acacia? When I named her? But ... that wasn't intended as a promise of love. I was just giving her a name."

"Aye, and what did you name her after?"

"A ..." David's jaw would have dropped clear down to his shoes, if it had been possible. "A flower. A golden flower."

"And that name has strengthened her. She's put up a bigger fight against the Shade in the last few days than I've ever seen her do before. So let's review, yes? She smelled the goodness in you. You gave her a name that she accepted. I'm fairly sure the oracle wasn't about me."

David rested his back against the tree, trying to organize his thoughts. He closed his eyes, and remained very still. He listened as a bird cried overhead, and as the wind rustled the leaves above. Yet this "listening" that the shaman had advised wasn't making him feel enlightened. In fact, he felt more confused than ever. Had Gullin already figured out all three parts of the riddle? Was he not telling David something? Had he known the whole time about what each "flower" was?

"Bast."

David was brought back from his contemplation by Gullin's soft-spoken word. "What?"

"Bast was the Egyptian cat goddess. She was highly revered and one of Egypt's most important deities." Gullin clasped his hands together, bringing them to his chin, as if in prayer. "That was the name I offered her."

The birds and the wind went silent at that instant, or so it seemed in David's mind. "You gave her a name? So, her real name is Bast?" A strange emotion gripped David, one that he couldn't tell was relief or dismay. "So you promised yourself to her first ..."

"I said I offered her that name. I didn't say she accepted it."

"She can reject a name?"

"Why should she have to accept it, if she doesn't like it?"

"But ... how do you know she rejected it? She couldn't come right out and say it."

Gullin's lip curled. "I told you, she and I used to chat regularly in our sleep. Frankly, I would've rather taken a claw gouging to the face than to hear her say 'no.'" He threw his hands up in casual defeat. "But, hey, there's no taming a lady's heart if it doesn't want to be caught, eh?"

David was once again thrown speechless. He rubbed the back of his neck. "I'm sorry, Gullin."

"What are you sorry for?" Gullin picked up a stick lying at his feet and twiddled with it. "Guess I should have given her the name of a flower. Had I known that's what that oracle meant the first time she told it to me, I would've named her after any flower she wanted."

"So you did know about the oracle already!" The mechanizations in David's brain processed what Gullin had just said. "She told *you* about the oracle? She didn't tell me about it. In fact, she said she didn't know how to do anything about the Shade." He couldn't help but feel betrayed by this revelation. "Why would she tell you about the oracle, and not me?"

Gullin shrugged.

"That means she thought you were the one the oracle was talking about," David concluded.

"Guess that's why she let me stay with the family to begin with. I think she was sure I was the one she was looking for." He shoved his sleeve down over his crest, as if the tattoo suddenly gave him shame. "Guess she lost faith in me after a while, when there was nothing I could do to get rid of that Shade. I can kill any other evil creature on earth, but not that."

Prickles nipped on the nape of David's neck. He suddenly did not want to be alone in the woods with this man, who was looking at him like he wanted to slice his throat. "Still, she told you the oracle, and never told me. If Acacia changed her mind and thinks *I'm* the one the oracle is talking about, then why did she not tell me?"

Gullin's fists were clenched so tightly, his hands were turning white. "Been trying to figure that one out myself. Best I can figure is because of the oracle's last line. She didn't mind me knowing it, guess because she doesn't care what happens to me in the end. She must feel a tad different about you."

"The last line?" David was quiet as he recited the last few lines of the oracle in his head. "The last line said, '*The Shade shall be imprisoned in stone.*' What's so unsettling about that? That's a good thing, isn't it?"

Gullin cocked an eyebrow at him. Both eyebrows rose up and he breathed an "ah" of realization. "I wondered why you didn't say the last line when you recited the oracle the first time. You don't know it. It didn't sound like something was missing, boyo? That the riddle just ended like that?"

"I thought maybe Hypnos didn't finish recreating the vision, or maybe the oracle had never been fully completed. But there was another line. And it's ... not good, is it?"

Gullin stood up, clearing his throat and he spoke in a steady voice. "The Shade shall be imprisoned forever in stone ... *Then shall Night claim the hero for her own.*"

A tree might as well have toppled onto David, for

that was the heavy brunt that he felt on him. "Night will claim the hero ... as in, darkness shall befall him?"

"Nyx is the Night. If someone were to defeat her Shade, and ruin all her plans, I think it'd be worse for the bloke than just 'darkness befalling him.' She'd flat out kill him, David boy. This oracle isn't talking about Acacia's savior. It's talking about her martyr."

"And Acacia didn't want me to know."

"She was trying to protect you. At least, after she—" Gullin fell silent, as he turned his head towards the direction of a rustling in the brush. David held his breath, as the rustling sounded like something heavy plodding their way.

His hair stood on end as a bear lumbered out from behind a tree, looking directly at them.

Gullin spoke in a whisper. "Don't move. Most times, these brutes don't want any more to do with us than we them. But if he charges, I'll handle him. You run to someplace safe."

David was going to ask how Gullin planned to "handle him" without any weapon, but he didn't get a chance. The bear was loping over to them, and David was already willing his feet to run. Gullin shot up from the log, raised his fists over his head and bellowed at the bear. Instantly, the bear froze in its tracks. It lowered its head, folding one of its paws over its eyes.

David blinked in surprise. "*Mi Dios*, Gullin. You frightened him."

"Why is the scary man yelling at me?" the bear whimpered in Japanese.

David let out a long breath. "It's all right. It's Tanuki."

Gullin cracked his knuckles. "Don't suppose I can still give him a good whooping."

"It's all right, Tanuki. You gave us a scare, looking like that," David called.

Tanuki the bear shambled over to David, panting heavily. "Sorry I took so long. When those men took you into that village, I was waiting to see what they would do to you. But I saw this bowl of vegetables by one of those funny houses, and I was soooooooooo hungry, but when I went to get one a mean old woman chased me with a stick. I hid until she went away, but by the time I thought it was safe to come out, they took you to this forest, so I followed after you, but then I got lost and a weasel chased me, but I changed into this shape to scare him away, and that was fun, and here I am now, and there you are, and there's the smelly man—"

"All right, Tanuki," David said. "I think we're all caught up now."

"We couldn't go anywhere without the fur-ball, now could we?" Gullin looked as if he had just bitten into something sour. "We ought to keep going. You can't finish this bloody spirit walk if we just stand around. Oh, and boyo, if you can talk to violets, or whatever that ridiculousness is, don't let me know. Keep it to yourself."

"Oh, I almost forgot," Tanuki added, "there was

this lady in white back there, right after I scared off the weasel. Funny thing, she must speak animal because I could understand what she was saying clear as day—"

"A lady in white?" David walked up to Tanuki. "What lady? What did she tell you?"

Tanuki shifted back into a badger. "She said I should take you to a clearing down this way, past a stream and a tree with a bee's hive. And she said only you could come, and the red-haired man should wait right here."

David recalled what the shaman had said. Ptesan-Wi was the White Calf, and supposedly female. If Ptesan-Wi passed between the bison and the people, undoubtedly she could take on a human form. This had to be the first sign of his vision. He had to go on alone, with his badger guide showing him the way. Given that this mysterious lady in white had been able to talk directly to Tanuki, there couldn't be a much clearer sign than that. He looked over at Gullin. "Gullin, Tanuki said that he was told by a woman in white to take me to a clearing. I think maybe it's Ptesen-Wi—"

"Well, that was quick, wasn't it? You *must* be special." Gullin sat back down on the log, crossing his legs to get comfortable. "Go on, boyo, this is where you go on by yourself. Old Gullin will be waiting for you. Make sure to come back with that stone. I'll be mighty sore if you don't."

David nodded, and he turned to Tanuki. "Well, Spirit Guide, lead the way."

CHAPTER FOURTEEN

If Nyx was the Night, she was not being compassionate. The shadows of dusk distorted the trees, and the calls of the nocturnal shattered the serenity of the forest like gunshots. Tanuki, able to see well in the dark, shifted back into a bear so that David could hold onto his fur and not get separated from him. As they walked, Tanuki sniffed the forest floor, gobbling up a mushroom whenever he came across one. David, despite not having eaten for a good while, was not hungry. He was too consumed with thinking about what he was heading towards, and what he had found out about the oracle. Was he really the "one" that the oracle had referred to? What if he wasn't? If he wasn't, would Ptesan-Wi help him, or, as the shaman had cautioned, would she destroy him? What if it was Gullin who was supposed to be doing what he was doing now?

He heard the gentle babbling of a stream not far ahead, and his heartbeat quickened. Tanuki stopped at the stream and took a good long drink. David, realizing he was parched, knelt down and took a handful of the refreshing water and drank.

"Would you like me to catch you a fish?" Tanuki asked. "We could build a fire and cook it."

"I'd rather we get to the clearing as quickly as possible," David answered.

"How about honey?" Tanuki insisted. "That lady said we'll pass by a bee hive on the way. I'm good at getting honey."

"If you want honey, go on and get it," David said. "Be quick, so we don't waste time."

Not too far past the stream, Tanuki's nose twitched and he licked his lips. "I smell it! I smell honey. It's up in that tree, right there."

David couldn't see anything, given the darkness. Tanuki shifted back into a badger and scrambled up the tree, leaving David alone in the darkness.

"Tanuki! Don't take too long," he called.

The wind whipped around him harder, and David hugged his arms around himself for warmth. He listened for any noises from the tree, but Tanuki had seemed to vanish.

"Tanuki, come back down," David shouted. No answer.

A bolt of lightning burst from overhead onto the ground not far from where David stood. He reeled back and stumbled over in shock, and as he lay there he tried gathering his composure and his wits. He spotted a light down the path, about where the lightning had struck. He considered whether or not to go to it. Had Tanuki caused that lightning bolt, as a kind of joke? Or was this part of his vision?

"Tanuki, can you hear me? I see a light down the path. Can you see it from up there?"

No answer.

David paused, scratching his head. "I'm going to go inspect that light. I won't go too far. Catch up with me," he called.

He crept down the path, advancing slowly towards the light. He could tell it was not a light from a fire, for it did not waver and was not the warm reddish-orange of flame. It was a steady bluish-white light, much like the kind he was often told one might see on their way to Heaven, and he wondered if this was a bad omen. When he finally reached the source of the light, it was radiating from something lying on the ground. The light softened as David approached it, enough so that he could make out what was lying there. Immediately he froze.

The light was coming from the bones of a skeleton. The skeleton was wearing the charred remains of Gullin's clothes.

David wanted to run. He wanted to find Tanuki and demand to be taken back through the Curtain. He wanted to go home. He wanted to wake up and find out this was a bad dream. Before he could take any action, he saw the outline of someone standing on the other side of the bones, the faintly illuminated face of a woman.

Oh God, oh God ... David was paralyzed. Was this ... Nyx?

The women stared at David. Long black hair braided with beads framed her face, and a long white shawl was wrapped around her body. Her feet were bare, but she wore bands of beads around her ankles.

David stammered, but his words formed as anger pushed its way through him. "You ... you did this? You killed him! He didn't deserve this!"

The woman smiled at him. Not a malicious smile—a motherly, gentle smile, not one that you would expect from someone dangerous.

"You'll pay for this!" David found himself shouting without control or caution.

The woman raised her hand. "Show no anger," she spoke softly. "Touch the bones."

David's breath caught in his throat. This woman was crazy. Would David incinerate too, if he touched the skeleton? All he could think of was: *This wouldn't have happened to Gullin, if I had never come here.*

"You must face what you fear," the woman said. "Touch the bones."

The young man wiped his hands over his face. What had he gotten himself into? All he had wished to do was find the Turquoise. He had wanted to banish the Shade of Nyx, and save Acacia ...

Acacia ...he could still save her. He couldn't let Gullin die for nothing. Even if this was madness, he was the only one left to fulfill the oracle. He had to get the Singing Turquoise, no matter what this woman was planning to do to him. He reached down and wrapped his fingers around the skeleton's right wrist—

He was holding a toy wooden sword.

"David! David, darling, come downstairs," he heard a lyrical voice calling him. "We have a surprise for you."

David stood up, looking around at the walls of a familiar room, with its yellow-striped wallpaper, light green drapes on the windows, and polished wooden furniture. Toys and books of all kinds littered the floor, and there was a welcoming bed with finely pressed sheets.

He was in his bedroom. He was home. After realizing he was shorter than usual, and looking over his clothes— that silly sailor-style suit his mother always made him wear—he discovered he was seven years old again.

"David, did you hear me, dear?" He heard his mother calling from the stairway out in the hall. "Stop playing with your toys and come downstairs."

David dropped the toy sword and scurried excitedly out of the bedroom and down the staircase, to the front parlor of his house. There his mother stood, in her blue dress that she wore fondly, with her dark hair up in a tight neat bun held in place with a tortoise shell comb. Next to her stood another woman, about eighteen years of age, wearing a plain lavender dress and holding a strangely-shaped black case in her hands. She had a bright smile, shining ebony eyes, and her mahogany-brown tresses were held back by a white lace scarf.

"David, this is Señorita Flores," his mother said. "She is going to be your tutor in music."

David rubbed the back of his right leg with his left foot. He held his hands behind his back, lowering his head, but his eyes never left the strange lady.

"Don't be rude, David. Come here and greet your new teacher," his mother commanded.

David shuffled over to the woman. She continued smiling her wonderful smile, and she made a short curtsy. "It's a pleasure to meet you, David. Your mother tells me you love to learn. We'll have so much fun together."

That was what all of David's teachers said. This one may have been prettier than the others, but he was sure she would be just as boring. He wanted to read the books he wanted to read, and not have to go through the boring lessons that his tutors forced him to do.

"Can I go play?" he asked his mother earnestly.

"Of course not. You're going to have your first music lesson. Sit and listen to Señorita Flores." His mother glided out of the room, shutting the parlor doors behind her.

David sat in a chair across the room from Miss Flores, who sat down on the couch. She patted the spot next to her. "Come now, no reason to be shy. If I'm going to be your music teacher, we should get to be friends."

David hesitated, but trundled over and sat on the couch. He looked at the odd case in her hands. "What's in there?" he asked.

Miss Flores opened the case, and pulled out a finely polished instrument. It resembled an enlarged violin. "This is a very special instrument. It's called a viola. I'm going to teach you how to play it, as well as the piano. I could also teach you the clarinet and the flute, if you'd like. But we'll start with this."

David felt disappointed. "I'd like to learn to play something else. That looks like no fun."

"Oh, but that's not true. The viola is the finest of the strings. It has a richer, fuller tone than a violin, and is more expressive and crisp than a cello. It is the life-giving breath of many great symphonies, and is beloved by the best composers. A violist is a very special person."

David touched the viola with one finger, as if testing it. "Do I have to?"

"Try it for a few weeks. If you don't like it, we'll move along to something else. But I can already tell, with those fine fingers of yours, you will be an excellent musician."

"Yes, Señorita Flores."

"You may call me Catarina, if you like. It'll be our secret." She winked at him.

No ... no, I don't want to see this! Why are you making me think about this? Are you trying to drive me mad? Please ... please just let me go ...

David was thirteen, going on fourteen. He had become knowledgeable in many things, and was already well known for his love of odd, magical tales. He was a fine violist now, regularly entertaining guests of the family who stayed at the house. He did not mind it; as a matter of fact, he enjoyed his viola lessons more than any other, even though his daily lessons had been shortened to weekly due to his other studies. He insisted to continue the lessons so he would be the best viola player in the country— and so that Miss Flores would keep coming over to the house.

Catarina had also taught him the piano over the years, but it was their special time with the viola that he looked forward to. The way she would lightly touch his fingers to correct his position on the strings, the way she would watch him with an enthusiastic light in her eyes when he played, the way she laughed like a bird's song when he would say something witty or funny. He absolutely loved his time with her.

Others in Cervera would sometimes make pitying remarks about Catarina. She was getting on in years, they said, and no eligible bachelor who had come to court her had asked for her hand. Most attributed it to her "peculiar demeanor," as she was often more outspoken than was proper. Rumor had it she also liked to do boyish things, like catch frogs by the river, and ride horses bareback. She would soon become a lonely spinster, they said, if she did not start behaving in a more acceptable manner.

David did not care. He liked Catarina for being so different. If no one ever asked for her hand in marriage, that would be fine. He'd make sure he took care of her. In fact, when he was old enough and had a good career, he'd buy her a house so she'd always have a place to stay. Better yet, he'd buy his own house and ask her to come live with him. Then they could play duets together all the time. He would show her the sonata he had been composing for the last several months. It was not quite right yet, but by her next birthday he would have finished it.

"Isn't it wonderful, David?"

David stared at her.

"I'll be moving to Barcelona in a few days. Alejandro has already acquired a grand house, and he wants to have the wedding there. It's not far away, so I can come visit every now and then." Her beautiful smile faltered, but she kept a cheerful attitude. "I know we won't be able to have our lessons, but you hardly need me anymore. You and your family can come up and visit us, too, whenever you wish. Alejandro has a gorgeous viola from Hungary that he says he has no interest in keeping, so I can have it sent to you once I get there, or you can come have it when you visit."

David forced himself to give Catarina a weak smile.

Catarina embraced him, but normally where her embraces felt like coming home after a perilous voyage, it now felt like a kiss from a guillotine. She noticed a roll of paper that David was holding behind his back. "What is that you have there?'

David clenched his fist around the manuscript paper. "It's nothing. Just a new song I was thinking about practicing."

"You'll have to make sure you learn it before our next visit, right?" She smiled again, and she kissed him lightly on the forehead.

At that moment, David wished that the roll of paper in his hand, the one with his finally finished sonata written on it, was a dagger. It might as well have been, because he felt one lodged in his back at the moment. The sonata ended up as kindling in the fireplace that night.

"David, what on earth happened?" His mother was somewhere between concerned and livid, it was hard to tell with her. She was staring at David's viola, which was smashed in half on the floor, barely held together by its ligaments of string.

David looked at her, his face a blank. "I dropped it," he replied dully.

His mother crossed her arms. "Don't think I'm a fool, David. First, you allow your brothers to use your old viola as a racket, and now you've destroyed this one that Catarina sent you. These instruments are expensive, David. I won't allow all those years we invested in your playing to be wasted because of your temperament. You should be happy for Señora Fernandez and her husband. Stop being so selfish."

David's body was as rigid as a crowbar. "I'm not going to play music ever again."

"Honestly, David, you must have known that you and she couldn't—"

"Did you hear what I said? You call this an 'investment,' but what would I ever use this for anyway? I know a hundred other things that are more practical. I don't need this." He stormed out of the room, slamming the door behind him.

David felt hot, yet he shivered. He was sitting in mud, and he was slowly sinking into it. He did not care. He had no energy or will to move. Rain pounded the earth around him, making the mud gelatinous and causing him to sink faster. Somehow, the mud felt good. David imagined himself as a frog, settling deep into the wet ground, out of sight, hidden from the rest of the world.

Actually, he was a frog. He was conscious of being a frog, but it did not matter to him. He nestled himself into his grimy surroundings, deciding this was a perfectly acceptable mode of living.

"Is this why you came here?" he was asked by a distant voice. "Because you want to keep running from who you are?"

The frog blinked.

"What good is all the knowledge you have gained, all the time you've spent learning, if you're just going to sink into the mud?"

The frog croaked, but did not move.

"How can you hope to save anyone else, if you won't save yourself?"

The frog was now almost completely submerged in the mud. The darkness and coolness were inviting. But, he did think: *How do I do that?*

"By accepting the balance of both the good and the misfortune in your life. Only by acceptance and forgiveness can we heal from wounds. If you can learn to heal, then you will be able to heal others. Is that not what you came here to do?"

It began to come back to David. He willed his stumpy legs to lift him up, but the mud sucked him back down. He forced his head above the mud, and with all the strength he could muster, he leapt up and out from the earth. For the briefest moment he felt suspended in the air … a clear, clean space of nothing, a neutral place without distraction or influence. He did not feel himself descend back down, for the next moment he was sitting cross-legged, with his human legs attached to his human body, on what felt like a lush woolly animal pelt. The pelt beneath him lifted ever so slightly, in a breathing rhythm. David wondered if he was seated atop something alive.

The woman in white was standing there before him. She placed one hand on David's head. With the other, she placed something small, round and cool in his hands, folding his fingers around them. She said nothing, but she leaned in and kissed David on the forehead, exactly like Catarina had before she had left.

This time, though, David did not feel resentment or anger. He was at peace.

The woman disappeared, and in her place was a white bison, looming over David. The pelt that David was seated on folded up around him, enveloping him in a gentle cocoon of fur until it melded into him. While David no longer saw the pelt, he could sense that it was still around him, an invisible barrier that made him feel safe and unafraid.

"Be on your way now," the White Calf said, and she was gone.

David was sitting alone in the clearing, as the sunrise sliced through the darkness as a golden blade of light. There were no bones, no mud, no bison. He looked down to see an apricot-sized turquoise stone glistening in his hands.

CHAPTER FIFTEEN

David walked back down the path through the woods, along the way finding a honey-coated Tanuki sleeping soundly at the base of a tree. He pocketed the turquoise stone, and carefully picked up Tanuki, who snorted in his sleep.

"Ey, boyo, you've been gone all night." Gullin, in perfect health although dirty and a bit sleep-deprived, was sitting on the same log. The dying embers of a small campfire fizzled at his feet, and next to it were leftover bits of a grouse that he had caught for a late dinner.

David was so happy to see Gullin alive, he almost dropped Tanuki. "Gullin! You're okay! I had a vision where you were a pile of bones!"

Gullin laughed brazenly. "Guess that explains how you feel about me."

David dug the Turquoise out of his pocket, holding it up. "I spoke to the White Calf. I passed her test."

Gullin let out a long whistle. "Looks like you did a good job, lad. So, how was the White Calf?"

"Beautiful but scary," David replied.

"Well, she is a woman," Gullin chuckled. "You can

tell me all about it on the way back. Wake up the gopher and let's get back through the Curtain."

It was much faster going back through the Curtain, for Tanuki had only to follow the scent of his Master Yofune. They exited the Curtain right at the entrance of Yofune's lair, and the trio found all the gypsies and Yofune safe and sound, and fast asleep.

"Master Yofune! Everyone! We found it! We have the Singing Turquoise!" David rushed over to the sleeping blind man, and tried to nudge him awake. "Master Yofune, wake up. I found the earth spirit, and she gave me the—"

He noticed the faint tinkling of bells coming from somewhere in the lair. He nudged Yofune again, but the sea dragon did not awaken. Everyone was in a comatose state, an almost death-like slumber. David heard something collapse behind him, and he turned to see Gullin and Tanuki lying in a heap on the floor, in the deepest sleep.

Of course, there had to be more trouble. David darted his gaze about, trying to see if there was an intruder in the cave. Panic seized him, as he realized: *If everyone's been asleep, then someone could have come in and done something to Acacia—*

He dashed over to the wagon where he had left Acacia, and threw open the door. At the other end of the wagon room, Acacia slept—she was sleeping, wasn't she? David ran to her, checking for any signs of life. She was still breathing, thank God, but hardly. She was withering away, every inch of her skin riddled with greenish-blue veins. He hoped he had returned in enough time. He removed the Turquoise from his pocket.

The tinkling of bells became louder, and the door of the wagon clicked shut behind him. He turned to see Nico standing inside the wagon, locking the door. A small shiny device was around Nico's neck, a tiny music box that trickled its droplets of noise like grains of the Sandman's sand.

"Hello, David," Nico greeted him with all the warmth of winter. "I was wondering where you had gotten off to. Do you like my latest trinket? A fancy little fairy gift. It does wonders to quiet a crowd."

David held tight to the Turquoise, lowering it out of Nico's view. "I don't have time for your nonsense, Nico. Get out of here."

"I'm afraid I can't do that. I'm here to collect, as per my agreement. I confess, I'm puzzled as to why my music box isn't working on you." Nico sniffed the air, and immediately gagged and covered his nose. "Blegh! That's one odorous protection spell you have on you. Smells like a dead festering horse."

David thought back to that strange invisible pelt that Ptesan-Wi had enveloped him in. She must have sensed that he would run into more danger and given him a ward against enchantments.

Nico advanced a few steps towards him, but David spun around, spreading his arms out to block the fox from Acacia. The Teumessian laughed. "Planning to stop me? This will be fun. I'll love to see the look on your face as you watch."

"Watch what? What did you mean, you've come to collect?" David demanded.

"In case you hadn't noticed, the Shade has taken about all it can from her," Nico said. "Whatever it was you were planning to do, you're too late. The Shade has come into maturity, so I'm here to harvest it and return it to its owner. My employer has been waiting many a century for her patience to pay off."

David gripped the stone tighter. "Nyx hired you to do this? You're working for her?"

Nico grinned. "No point in keeping it a secret, I suppose. How do you think that Shade got inside my cousin in the first place?"

The shocked, then disgusted expression on David's face encouraged Nico to expound with delight. "Madam Nyx's Shades, when they are first created, are almost undetectable. One can easily slip one into a wine goblet, and a sphinx wouldn't know she swallowed it until it was already embedded deep inside her. An easy task for a more than ideal arrangement: I help Nyx obtain a sphinx's wit, and with my cousin dead, I become the cleverest mind in the world. That is, short of Nyx herself, but I'm not competing with gods. Being the most ingenious brain among mortals is fine with me."

"You're not ingenious. You're sick," David hissed.

"And you're naïve, if you think you're any threat to me," Nico answered coolly. "As I said, there isn't anything you could do now to help your darling anyway. So if you'll be so kind and step out of my way."

From an inside pocket of his coat, he removed something that glinted in the dim light of the room. It was the sharpest, wickedest pair of scissors David had ever seen.

The scissors dropped out of Nico's hand as David delivered him a solid punch to the face that sent him reeling backwards, landing on his tail.

Nico was stunned, and he pressed his fingers to his bloody nose. His poised demeanor was rapidly replaced by his canine instinct, as his orange eyes flared and his teeth clenched into a vicious growl. A layer of copper-reddish fur spouted all over his skin, and his fingernails grew into long sharp points. His face distorted into something far more canine than man, and his lips pulled back in the same frightening way that Acacia's did when she was enraged. The visible patches of skin around his eyes and lips blackened to pitch, and his ears lengthened and tapered into points, stripping the last recognizable human trait from him. The fox beast rolled up onto all fours, crouching in preparation to lunge. "You're dead meat," he growled in a completely different, sinister voice.

David brought the Turquoise over his shoulder, preparing to throw it at Nico's head. But he couldn't risk losing the stone just to save himself. He saw Nico's scissors lying on the floor, and scrambled to get them. Nico was faster, jumping in front of him and swatting the scissors across the floor towards the door. David dealt him a crushing kick to the chest. Nico tumbled onto his back, and David leapt over him to dive after the scissors again. The fox beast twisted around, snagging David by the ankle and sending him flat down onto his stomach. He pounced on David's back and sank his teeth into his right shoulder. The boy screamed at the intense pain, trying to pry Nico off. Nico scratched him across the right cheek, and slammed his head against the floor. David lay there, half conscious and bleeding.

Nico wiped a trail of blood from his lip. He got up, snatching the scissors from the floor. He turned a wicked eye on David. "I really should test the sharpness of these first," he said. "I'd hate to be working with a set of dull blades." He snapped the blades like the jaws of a Jenglot.

David struggled to get on his feet, but Nico swooped down and snatched him by the wrist of his wounded arm. He yanked the boy halfway up off the floor, so David dangled from Nico's grip as the pain in his shoulder burned hot and raw. The fox paused for a moment, soaking in the anguish and horror on David's face. "This isn't a bedtime story. You're no hero. There wasn't any chance you were ever going to outwit me."

Nico noticed that David was still gripping the turquoise stone in his hand, despite the pain in his arm. The fox attempted to pry open the boy's fingers to get a good look at what this precious stone might be, but David would not relent. He tightened his fingers harder around the stone, but the feeling in his hand was beginning to numb.

"There's something special about your little rock," Nico mused. "If you're not going to let go, I'll have to snip those nasty little fingers off." He brought the serrated blades of the scissors towards David's hand.

David winced, clenching his teeth. He had lost. He lost the fight, he lost Acacia, and he was about to lose the Turquoise. He closed his eyes, clutching the stone, refusing to give it up even in the face of agony. He heard an odd little clinking noise, and he had the faint sensation of something tapping his knuckle.

"What on earth is that supposed to be?" he heard Nico spit in astonishment.

David ventured to open one eye to look. Nico's scissors were trying to bite down on his index finger, but were unsuccessful due to a sudden sheen that coated David's entire right hand. It was glossy blue-green, and hard as rock. It felt like an iron glove was fused to his hand. Nico gawked at the miraculous coating. He stabbed at it with the scissors, but it only caused the tips of the blades to bend.

David wrenched his hand out of Nico's grasp, and with a desperate lunge slammed his stone-plated fist into the side of Nico's leg. The force of the blow made Nico buckle, bringing him down onto his knee. David smacked Nico on his already broken nose, amplifying the pain. The sheer surprise of it made the fox drop the scissors. In an instant, the scissors were in David's one hand, and the end of Nico's tail was in the other.

Snip.

Nico shrieked as a good six inches of his tail were hacked off. He bolted across the room, howling and yelping and gnashing his teeth, while his butchered tail left a spattering of dark red spots on the floor. David staggered to his feet, clutching the scissors in one hand and the chunk of Nico's tail in the other. The fur on the Teumessian's head and neck bristled up, and his muscles tensed at the sight of his once magnificent tail now mangled.

David held the scissors out, the damaged points directed straight at Nico's face. His arms and legs wobbled, for the blood loss from his wound was making him weak. Nico saw this, and it only whetted his appetite. He charged right at David, teeth bared and claws extended. David reared his arm back to thrust the scissors with all of his strength, but as his attack went forward, his body went backwards from Nico slamming him against the wagon's door.

Both opponents were dead still, eyes locked, and neither was certain who might have just received a fatal blow.

David's mouth opened, but made no noise. Nico had him gripped with bone-wrenching strength by the shoulders, and the fox's claws were digging deep into his already dreadful shoulder wound. He looked down, for he still held the scissors. The handle end of it butted up against his chest, while the lethal end was digging into Nico. But there was no blood. Instead, the scissors had impaled the music box hanging from Nico's neck. The box's cylinder tumbled out, plinking onto the floor, rendering the music box voiceless.

Nico observed his dumb luck, and his lips drew back into a demonic smile. He laughed with pure joyful insanity. "I told you, I can't get caught," he sneered.

His smile abruptly dropped as a lioness's paw grasped him by the hair from behind.

The sphinx was fully awake, released from the music box's spell of slumber. Her growl of rage made Nico emit a small, helpless whimper. He was yanked back with such force, his spine bent backwards nearly to the point of snapping in half. David, released from the fox's grip, slumped to the floor in exhaustion. He felt a cold sensation over his hand as the glossy sheen retracted, resuming its stone state in the palm of his hand. He watched Acacia thrash Nico with unbridled ferocity. It was no contest for a lion, even an ill one, to fight a fox.

"I give! I give!" Nico gasped through Acacia's grinding grip on his throat. The sphinx was a terrible sight, the deathly pallor and gauntness of her face making the fury in her eyes all the more menacing. Nico gagged and choked, as Acacia pushed him down onto his knees and bent him backward. She grasped his scalp with her free paw and dug in her claws until he yelped.

Acacia looked back at David. Seeing and smelling the blood that had stained the right side of his shirt intensified her feral madness. Her lips pulled back, exposing teeth and gums. She gaped open her jaws to clamp onto Nico's face and crack his skull.

"Acacia ..."

The sphinx stopped. David slowly arose, leaning against the wall for support. He was pale and exhausted. "Acacia ...you don't have to do that. He's the monster. You're not."

Acacia's murderous wrath softened into curious bewilderment.

"You're more important than he is. He's not worth it. All I want to do now is help you." As much as he loathed to say it—he really wouldn't have minded watching Acacia shred Nico a while longer—he said, "Get him out of here."

Acacia turned her gaze back to Nico, who was shivering in terror. A small grin escaped her. She dragged the Teumessian by the hair across the wagon, unlocked the door, and threw him outside, shutting the door behind him.

Nico, blinking in confusion at being released so easily, pushed himself up into a sitting position. He observed his snipped tail, and tried to fold the remaining fur over to taper the end. His attention turned from his tail to the crowd of infuriated gypsies surrounding him. Everyone was wide awake and glowering at him, including the Huntsman, an abnormally large gorilla of a badger, and one extremely fuming, growling sea dragon.

"Fox hunting season is open, everybody," Gullin said, gleefully cracking his knuckles.

CHAPTER SIXTEEN

With a quick slice of her claw, Acacia tore a length of cloth from a drape hanging on the wagon wall. Even though she was barely able to stay on her feet, she set David down on the bed cushion, and pulled back his shirt collar so she could see his shoulder wound. Her natural instinct was to lick the puncture to clean it, but she could hardly touch the wound without David wincing and jerking away. She wrapped his wound as best she could with the drape cloth to stop the bleeding. The exertion from the fight and her anxiety to tend to David's injury caught up with her, and she collapsed against his chest.

"Acacia, stay awake! If you fall asleep, you might …" David did not want to think of it. He lifted up the Turquoise in his left hand. "I got the Singing Turquoise. I can banish the Shade from you."

The sphinx tilted her head up, blinking wearily at the Turquoise. It was as if she did not understand, or maybe she had lost any hope of salvation so did not believe him. He put her down on the cushion, kneeling beside her. He held the stone in both hands, and gently laid it on her stomach, since that was where her pain stemmed from.

There was a long silence, as David realized he had no idea what to do. The stone did not appear to be doing anything, so he put his hands back over it and concentrated hard, focusing his thoughts into directing the stone to banish the Shade. Acacia lifted her head to watch his meditation, but she furrowed her brow. After several minutes of this, to no effect, David reached back into his knowledge of folklore to figure out what to do. He tried commanding the stone in Spanish, English, Latin, Japanese, and every language he could recall from his studies. He tried an impromptu spell in rhyme, he tried placing the stone on various areas of Acacia's body, and he turned the stone over and over in his hands to find any secret, any hidden symbol or crack that would indicate what should be done. Nothing.

David couldn't understand. Had Ptesan-Wi tricked him, and given him a false Singing Turquoise so he would not find the real one? But this stone did have powers, given that it had protected his hand from being severed. Was there a special trick he had to do first? Out of desperation, he tried smashing it open on the floor, as if the secret was buried inside of it, but the stone was unbreakable. He clenched his teeth in frustration, resting his head in his hands as he tightened his fist on the stone.

He felt Acacia's paw touch his knee. She was looking at him, a sad smile on her face. "*Nullus Metus*," she whispered. She reached over, taking his hand with the stone and placing it down on the cushion beside him. She managed to crawl so she could put her head in his lap, and she sighed a very faint purr before shutting her eyes.

"Do not fall asleep!" David pleaded. "Please, Acacia … give me a second to figure this out. I could go back and find Ptesan-Wi again, and ask her how to make this work. I need a little more time, that's all. Acacia …"

He cradled the sphinx in his arms, looking into that wild but beautiful face. She looked so frayed; she hardly seemed beastly in any way now. He brushed her hair away from her face. "I tried. I really did. But I must have misunderstood the oracle. I just … I don't know what else I can do. I'm sorry. There must be something I missed, something …"

Acacia reached up, softly turning his face to look at her. Her eyes glowed that soothing, welcoming shine, an invitation to sleep.

"Wait, I …" David started. The hypnosis was already having its effect. Before he could argue, he slumped backwards onto the cushion, the sphinx held in his arms, as his mind crossed onto the plane where they could be together for one last time.

Catarina's face lit up as David showed her the patch of violets in the garden. "They're beautiful, David." She knelt down, inhaling the flowers' fragrance. They were taking a stroll on his family's estate, since she had decided they could have their lessons outside that day, given the warmth and sunshine. This was a well deserved respite.

"I know you like them." David beamed. He had especially asked his mother to have the violets planted in the garden that year, for Catarina. While it was a romantic cliché to give a girl flowers, he did not have the funds to do anything more impressive. Catarina enjoyed the simple things, and he knew she liked violets. When the violets would fully bloom, he'd have a bouquet cut so Catarina could take them home.

"I do like them, very much. Have I ever told you why?"

David thought about it. "Is purple your favorite color? You wear purple often."

"It is one of my favorites. But, actually ... you'll find this silly. It's the violet's name."

"That's not silly. Violet is a nice name."

"Not that, exactly. It's because violets are in the viola family of flowers, like my favorite instrument. Every time I see a violet, I hear beautiful music."

"I know what you mean." He, too, always heard beautiful music when he saw the most beautiful being in the world.

"All of this flower talk, it must bore you."

"No. Nothing you talk about bores me."

"You're a sweet man, David. Let's return to your lesson." She held his hand for a brief moment as they turned to head back towards the patio, but that moment uplifted David as nothing had before in his entire life. It was also the first time someone had called him a man, and not a boy. He wouldn't have traded that moment for all the wealth or all the fame in the world.

David returned from the memory, still feeling the pangs of sadness and the blissful joy that reliving that moment gave him. He knew Acacia had especially selected for him to remember that time. She had sorted through his thoughts and brought it into full clarity. Why? What had been so special about that? Had she always been picking through his memories every time that they connected in dreams? Oddly, it embarrassed him that Acacia knew about Catarina. Not that there was any reason why he should be embarrassed, but Acacia must have known how painful it was for him to think of *her* …

You shouldn't be sad. That was a nice memory.

David was in his family garden again, but not in the memory. He was his current sixteen-year-old self, although his wounds were gone, and his clothes were clean and pressed. Down the stone pathway walked the human form of Acacia, wearing a crisp white summer dress trimmed with a peach sash at the waist and pinkish lacing at the hem of the skirt and edges of the sleeves. She smiled at him, but even in this place of dreams, the smile was faded with fatigue and infirmity.

"That's an unusual choice of dress for you," David noted.

Acacia looked down at her dress. *I wanted to know what it was like, to live in the world you come from. This is an awfully cumbersome thing to wear.*

David walked over to her. "Why are you creating all of this? Why did you just show me that memory of … her?"

I recall the first time I tried to pull out one of your memories, back when you tried to leave the caravan. You've worked so hard on burying your thoughts about that woman, because all you ever focus on is the pain of loss. You allow that to overpower all the years of cheer and friendship that you felt learning from her. You mourned for the loss of your happiness, rather than rejoice in the awakening of hers. I wanted to remind you, for that one painful memory, you've got hundreds, thousands more of good, joyful ones. Both joyful and painful memories teach us something for the better. It's like when a musician plays a gorgeous song, and plays one sour note. Should that one bad note ruin the rest of the song? Or should he keep playing right on through to the end, and remember the next time he plays, he needs to pay more attention to play it perfectly?

David was quiet while he took in her words. He shook his head. "Pain stamps a much more lasting scar in your mind than joy."

I didn't say it doesn't hurt. Trust me, I know, she

243

admitted. *Loss isn't foreign to me. And it won't be the last time you will feel that way. You will face it all your life. But that doesn't mean you have to hide from living your life, by becoming buried in lessons and work, with no time for being yourself. The answer you're looking for is not written in a book, or hidden in the moral of a fable.*

"What answer? I don't even know the question."

Acacia touched the tip of his nose with her finger. *Remember, the answer is in the world around you. In the people you'll meet, and the people you'll part from. Don't try to make your goodbyes permanent.*

"Why ..." He wanted to ask more, but he realized that Acacia was giving her last few moments to him, to give him a lesson she knew was important. It meant as much to her as to him that he take her words to heart. This was her parting gift, the last piece of her special wisdom that she could pass on. "Thank you," he replied.

Acacia sat down on an iron-wrought bench next to a flower bed. *I know you wanted to ask why I was telling you all of that. A sphinx can only hope that she's fulfilled her purpose, that she's enlightened someone before she becomes the desert sand. But I was also hoping, for that small piece of advice, you could return the favor.*

David waited, unable to imagine what he could do for her now.

I don't have much time, she said, *but I would like you to play me that song you wrote. The one you were going to play for her. The one you never got to show anyone.*

"I … it's been a while …"

I know if I asked you to play it in the waking world, your mind would be inhibited by lack of memory and practice. But here, in your dream, I can help piece together your memories of when you originally wrote it. You can remember it as if you just freshly composed it. You can show me how it would have sounded in your most ideal way, any way your mind can design. I would like that.

"Why would you want to hear that?"

It's all I really want, at this moment.

David paused, and he concentrated as he could gradually feel tidbits of his composition flow back into his thoughts, scattered traces of memory knitting themselves back together. He recalled all the hours he poured into meticulously dotting each note on the manuscript paper, replaying each bar of music until he had polished it into a gem, crafting the melodies as his bow caressed each string to produce its rich tone. The song reconstructed itself back into its original tapestry, and when it was completed, he saw that a beautiful viola was waiting patiently in his hands.

Acacia smiled up at him, folding her hands in her lap. She really did look quite beautiful, although David had become accustomed to the wild feline features that made her unique. He honestly wished that this was not the last request of a dying friend. Acacia could sense his sadness, but she gestured at him with both hands. *Please play*, she urged.

As soon as David laid the bow to the viola, coaxing forth the first note he had brought to life in a long time, the dreamscape around them reacted to his music. At first, he barely noticed it. He was caught up in the memory of his long-lost song, surprised at himself that he had composed something so intricate and grand. Soon, it dawned on him that the dream surrounding him was contributing, that a choir of soft strings and woodwinds was whispering in accompaniment to his melody. Each note of his song produced a color, a splash of light that enhanced the spectrum of the garden, until the garden was shifting into something far more fantastic. The orchestra that David was imagining blossomed to include brass and percussion, while his viola sang out proudly. The story of the song came to life in vibrant imagery: a young warrior with sword in hand, quested across forests and deserts and oceans, riding on the backs of stallions, sailing on a great dragon-headed Viking ship, and flying through the air in a chariot pulled by bronze-feathered eagles. He swam through dark waters, guided by bioluminescent fish that glowed blue and green and yellow. He scaled mountains with caves of gold and jewels guarded by goblins. He fought giants who rose out of the earth in a mass of moss and stone, and defeated fierce rival knights with horned helmets. At the end of this orchestral quest, waiting for the young warrior on a grassy shore under a small birch tree overlooking a shimmering sea, was a dark-haired woman in a flowing lavender dress. But as the music reached the last few bars of the song, the dress faded into white, and the woman's hazel eyes deepened in color to a golden-rimmed green …

David woke up.

The lingering strands of music resonated in his mind, but his brain adjusted as he remembered where he truly was. He looked at the interior of the wagon, and felt the softness of the cushion under him. He was holding Acacia in his arms, who had not awoken with him. She was still, her head against his chest, her frail body snuggled close to him. He palmed the cool Turquoise in his hand, quietly cursing this useless hunk of rock for having given him a false hope—

Although, had it always been carved to look like a coiled-up sleeping lizard? He swore it had been perfectly smooth before.

Acacia let out a long, deep sigh.

"Acacia?" David sat up, cradling her. "Acacia, are you all right?"

The sphinx slowly blinked her eyes open, and coughed lightly. She looked hazily around the room. She very weakly said, "*Bellus.*" Beautiful.

Her eyes opened up wide. She placed her paw on her stomach, wrinkling her forehead. She took a deep breath, and then very tentatively said something, not in Latin, but in the ancient Egyptian with which she had summoned the desert winds. Her lips did not pale, nor her flesh wither. With each word, her skin regained more of its tan hue, her hair its soft dark brown ochre. She spoke a few hesitant words of French ... then German, then Spanish, then what sounded like Chinese, and Russian. Her caution erupted into joy as she snapped her body up straight, and with renewed energy she jumped up, jabbering in a string of various languages, laughing and speaking more rapidly by the second. David sat there, mystified, until Acacia grabbed him by his arms and lifted him to his feet. She was giggling like he had never heard; her eyes bright as suns.

"You wonderful, brilliant man!" she cried, grasping David by his wrists and swinging him about. The young man noticed then that there was no more pain in his right shoulder, and as Acacia swung him about, the bandage dropped down and he could no longer see any trace of a wound.

"It's gone! I'm free!" She nuzzled her face into his roughly, unable to control her strength. "I'm free! I ... I'm fine," she said, calming herself down at seeing David's startled reaction. "I'm fine. Thank you, you've freed me from that awful thing." She nuzzled David's face again, more gently this time. She, too, saw that his injury had vanished. "And managed to help yourself, in one stone's throw, so to speak."

"But ... but how?" David was thrilled to see Acacia alive and well, and above that speaking without any pain. "I mean, the stone wasn't doing anything before ..."

"The Singing Turquoise is a healing stone," Acacia said. "But the power is not in the stone itself. It can only channel the power of the one who holds it. That strength came from you, David. It was all you. Your special voice." She chuckled. "My, it feels strange to be speaking a modern tongue again."

"My special voice?" It had only now clicked for him. "The oracle … '*The violet plucked will release his special voice.*' It wasn't talking about a literal violet … violets are in the viola family. That's why you showed me that memory of Catarina. It meant the viola! 'Plucked' meant plucking the viola's strings, not picking a flower. You figured that out a long time ago."

Acacia smirked, releasing David's wrists. "A sphinx does not reveal her secrets."

"Of course, that was why you had all those instruments in your nest! You were looking for the right instrument to cure you."

Acacia tilted her head at him. "You were snooping around in my bed?"

David blushed. "No, not exactly … Tanuki was burrowing in your bed … I mean, it's a nice bed and all, but he thought it was kind of lumpy … wait, that's not quite …" Acacia put a paw to his lips. David let out his breath. "I find it hard to imagine that you've never found a musician who could help you before now."

"You mean find a musician who wouldn't lose his mind at seeing a living, breathing sphinx? Or one who was foolish enough to seek out an ancient spirit to get the Singing Stone?" She grinned while raising an eyebrow at him. "It couldn't be just anyone, you know. It had to be someone who wasn't afraid. Someone who was meant to free me."

David smiled from ear to ear. "So you're going to be all right now?"

"Yes, yes … I'm still a little weak," she admitted, "but I'll get my strength back. I like that I can talk to you when we're awake," she added, and she started laughing again until she could barely breathe. "I like that I can talk! And I like that I can laugh! And I like …" She cut herself off. She was staring directly into David's eyes.

"I like it too," David said, and then he dropped his gaze. "We should let the others know that you're all right."

"Yes, we should." Acacia did not move. "Or, we can let them have a little more quality time with Nico. Before I shred him to bits." She flexed her claws. "David, I am so terribly sorry I put you through all of this."

"It was nothing," David casually replied, with a wave of his hand. "It's what we valiant types do." He paused, but his curiosity got the better of him. "Why did you ask me to play you my song? Wouldn't any song have done?"

Acacia bit her lip. "I really did want to hear you play it, no matter what might have happened. Honestly, I didn't know that the Singing Turquoise could channel your music in a dream. I'm sure Hypnos had a hand in it." Her smile crumbled, and she crossed her arms as her face became serious. "You need to go home now."

David was taken aback by the abrupt statement. "But … Gullin said there are rules about seeing the other side of the Curtain—"

Acacia shook her head. "It wouldn't be the first time my bloodline has forgone the 'rules.' We can make an exception. Most likely you'll wake up tomorrow and convince yourself you imagined it all."

"Do you want me to go home?" David hoped she would give some explanation for her decision.

"It's not a matter of want."

"What about the whole 'engagement'? I gave you a name. You accepted it."

"I told you, it's not binding. I release you from any misunderstood promises."

David couldn't help but feel dejected by her sudden turn of coldness. "I do have my apprenticeship in Paris. And my parents will be worried if they find out how long I've been gone. But we don't have to hurry back so soon. I'll invent a story for my absence. Maybe you could show me more through the Curtain …"

"No. I'll get Yofune to take you to a safe place outside of Paris. I will give you some money to complete your trip. I will arrange for the belongings you left behind to be returned to you." She turned and walked to the door of the wagon.

David felt a tearing in his chest. "Why the sudden rush to be rid of me?"

Acacia paused with her paw on the door. "You've done more than you needed to do. If you were here because of the oracle, or destiny, then you've fulfilled your purpose. You've helped me fulfill my purpose, too. But this isn't the world you were meant for. You must go back." She threw open the door of the wagon.

Both Acacia and David gaped dumbfounded as the door opened up not to Yofune's undersea lair, but a dark expanse of space, stretching out to eternity. As far as they could see was the clearest, purest midnight, speckled with diamond-mimicking stars and hundreds of full, porcelain-smooth moons hanging like lanterns in various colors. It was all so still, so untainted in its clarity and serenity, that it did not feel quite real.

Acacia tried to slam the door shut, but then the walls and floor of the wagon fell away, fading off into nothingness. They were standing on the top of a precipice, with broken columns of stone arising around them, and the ground they stood on was a polished surface with archaic symbols carved into it. Below, constellations swirled downwards into what appeared to be an inky whirlpool. Beyond the blackness, there was the faintest hint of light from the other side, but it was muddled from the swirling of the abyss. All around, various stars moved together in the shapes of dancers, animals, and strange creatures, all to the rhythm of some music that could not be heard.

"What just happened?" David managed to say. "Where are we?"

Acacia was pale, but not from any Shade blight— from panic. "I couldn't get you safely away fast enough," she whispered, taking hold of David's arm in a tight grip.

A heavy mantle of frost washed over them, and David knew they were not alone. There was a presence here, one he couldn't decipher yet, but out of the blackness of sky he could see a form coming towards them. All he could make out was the long trail of wispy smoke that flowed around the figure, the penetrating eyes of silver, and the enormous wings of glossy obsidian that were far too large for the feminine frame that supported them.

David did not need to ask who this shadowy figure was. He knew it was the one responsible for all of Acacia's years of suffering. The one who had killed other magical beings in order to steal their gifts.

Acacia bared her teeth at this menacing force approaching them. "It's as the oracle foretold. She's come for you."

CHAPTER SEVENTEEN

"Acacia, wait!" David whispered, as the sphinx prepared to lunge at the descending goddess of night. "Don't do something you'll regret. She could kill you."

"She's been doing that for most of my life," Acacia pointed out, snarling.

"I know she's put you through a lot of pain, and you want revenge—"

"Revenge would be a secondary satisfaction," the sphinx hissed. "It's hardly why I'll rip her throat out if she dares to come near you."

David had not forgotten the last line of the oracle. Nyx was coming to claim the one who saved Acacia from the Shade. It was why Acacia had tried to speed David away to safety, back to Paris in the modern civilized world where ancient goddesses held no authority. Attempting to outsmart or outrun a prophecy, however, had proven to be futile.

At the top of each column, a glowing orb popped into life, radiating a bluish-purple glow. The light cast a clearer picture on the environment they were in. David had seen pictures before of this kind of place. In ancient Greek and Roman temples, there was often a small room kept from the public where a cult image of a god was kept, reserved for priests and acolytes. This place reflected such an adyton, and now he could see a pedestal at one end of the floor surrounded by a pool of water. As soon as he saw the pedestal, the dark shape of their host alighted onto it, like a great vulture upon a perch.

David did not want to look at her, but he knew he had to. He watched with fear as the large glossy wings unfolded, spreading open until they enveloped all of the adyton. Exposed from her feathery cocoon was a woman of infinite beauty, her raven hair cascading down in a waterfall of lush locks, her skin as pale as moonlight, her face as fine as gleaming marble. Her eyes had all the soul-piercing glamour of a dream, but behind them was the icy gloom of a heart-stopping nightmare. Her body was swathed in a wispy indigo essence, which trailed off down her legs into a flowing twisting train of a gown that made it appear that she had no feet. She had the hint of a smile, but that little hint was more deadly than venom.

David was too awestruck by the goddess before him to react. Acacia stared wide-eyed at Madam Nyx, who in many ways looked like the sphinx, only rather than a feral cat-like exoticness, the goddess was raw power, an ethereal beauty that could will even the coldest heart to desire her. Acacia growled fiercely, pulling David behind her to guard him from the malicious presence before them.

Nyx eyed David, with a gaze that froze him in place. She held out her hand towards him. "Return my Shade to me."

David realized he still had the Singing Turquoise. He hesitated, but he knew that it was a bad idea to keep a primordial deity waiting.

"You have rendered my Shade useless in that stone. It is imprisoned forever. Even I cannot remove it. But it is mine. You will return it to me." Nyx kept her hand out, unwavering.

David stepped out from behind Acacia, who gave a soft whimper of warning. He advanced as far towards Nyx as he felt was safe. He placed the Singing Turquoise on the floor before her, and quickly retreated a few paces.

With a flick of her index finger, Nyx summoned the stone to rise into the air and come to rest in her palm. She tightened her hand around it, and lowered her arm. She returned her attention to her guests. "I have not brought mortals to my home for many a century. However, it is necessary that I deal with you. I have been waiting patiently for a long time to gather the essence of the world's last living sphinx. Such a creature's will is practically impenetrable, and only the strongest of my Shades could stand a chance to break it. I hardly have the strength now to begin the process over again."

David should have been focused on Nyx's threat,

but instead he looked over at Acacia. "You're the only sphinx left? In the whole world?"

Acacia gave him a look that said, *I can't believe you're concerned with that just now!*

David turned back to Nyx, a swell of bravery encouraging him to speak. "You would kill the last sphinx on earth, to have her knowledge? You've brought about the deaths of many just to have their talents. Why would you do that? I thought gods were supposed to be perfect already."

There was ice in Nyx's stare. Despite David's audacity, she spoke with continued calmness. "I have grown weaker in my time," she confessed, "and my current cycle of existence is drawing to a close. Thus I have been procuring the needed skills and gifts from the remaining creatures of the unseen world. There is no species, from your world or any other, that lasts forever. Their special gifts would die out, to be lost to time. I only wish to acquire them for my heir."

David was struck dumb for a moment. "Your … heir, Madam Nyx?"

Nyx pulled back a flowing fold of her gown, like a cascade of water ebbing away from shore. Within the chasms of her gown, a small being was revealed, a fragile boy who appeared no more than ten years old. He had the same dark hair and fine features as the goddess, and two of the tiniest gray wings emerged from his shoulder blades. Yet there was an emptiness to his eyes, as if he was lost. He was gaunt and frail, a fledging unable to leave his nest.

David regarded the boy, who glanced back briefly, before his empty eyes wandered off. "You have many children, Madam Nyx, so I am told. Surely you could have chosen someone like Hypnos as your beneficiary, and not had to go through the trouble of harming so many innocents?"

A gentle laugh escaped Nyx's throat. "This young child is not my son. He is my incarnation. He is what will be left of me once my current form flickers out of existence. He is my legacy. So as you can understand, he is much more valuable to me than a son or daughter."

David looked at the boy again, with newfound respect and dread. It was amazing to think that the tiny boy sitting there, seeming so detached, would grow to be as powerful as Nyx herself. But now he understood why Nyx was collecting the best traits from the magical world's finest. Her incarnation had not turned out the way she had planned.

"Odd that you mention my son Hypnos," Nyx continued. "After all this time, he has finally proven helpful to me. For, you see, he may guard the realm of Sleep, but I am its ultimate overseer. Through him, I was able to see how you used the dream to free the sphinx from my Shade. Unusual, I admit. I believe no one else would have possessed the ability to use a Singing Stone in that manner. But you have always had a profound connection to your dreams, David. I've seen quite a few of them for some time now."

The color drained from David's face. "You've been watching me?"

"I watch many. But, yes, you in particular I have kept an eye on. The events that have led you here were no coincidence." She turned her gaze to Acacia. "It is delightful to see you again, Acacia. I imagine you haven't recognized me yet."

Acacia tilted her head to the side, in bafflement.

Nyx shifted her form into one of an older woman, wearing the white outfit of a priestess. The orbs of the room shifted their light to a warmer, yellow light. The new Nyx looked almost inviting, a grandmotherly figure.

Nyx's changed appearance had a quick effect on Acacia. The fur on the back of her neck bristled, and her eyes widened. "No … you! It was you! Why … you deceived me!"

David shot his eyes back and forth between the two creatures. Before he could even ask, Nyx returned to her true appearance and said, "I did not deceive you. Has not everything in the oracle I told you come to pass? Did I not foretell that there was one who would free you from my Shade? Don't think I gave you that oracle in jest. I cannot change what is meant to be. I was deeply enraged to foresee the events that would unfold, that I had not looked farther into the future to see how all my efforts on you would go to waste."

Nyx was the priestess that gave Acacia her oracle? David thought, stunned. *Then that means ...*

"No, I did not design the oracle, or its outcome," Nyx answered David's thoughts. "But it has foretold of one prospect that is within my power to control." She floated down from her pedestal, hovering atop the pool of water. "I lost a lifetime's worth of work and waiting because of you, and there was nothing I could do to stop it. Even though I tried to indirectly intervene by employing Nico to my cause, I could not alter what I had prophesized. But I have also seen what course of action I am allowed to take with you."

Acacia lunged between David and the goddess, snapping her teeth at Nyx and growling a sincere threat. "You will not claim him! All that will come of harming him, is my devoted promise to make you suffer!"

Nyx shook her head. "Love does make even the most intelligent of creatures blind and stupid. There is nothing you can do to protect him. You are strong, but you are merely mortal. My oracle has already predicted that I will claim him. This is what is meant to be. If I cannot alter events, neither can you."

"No! I can do something about it!" Acacia turned her back to Nyx, and embraced David in a bone-cracking hug. She spread her wings, as if it would be an impenetrable wall. "Because you couldn't predict everything! You didn't say anything about how he'd risk his life for someone he barely knows, because it was the right thing to do. Or how he'd save my family from Nico. Or that I would …" She paused, as she tried to beat back the emotion rising up in her. Her voice got very quiet, oozing malice. "You can't take him. I won't let you."

David's thoughts were going in about a million different directions at that moment. The one he kept coming back to was that if Acacia stood in Nyx's way, she would be killed. David whispered to the sphinx, "Acacia, it's all right. Let me go."

Acacia looked at David with tearful eyes. "What? No! No, you've done nothing to be punished like this!"

"Acacia, let go of me."

The sphinx went rigid, but she relinquished. David walked past her and stepped towards Nyx. "Madam Nyx, if your intent is to claim me, then you can have me. But you must promise that you will not harm Acacia or her family in any way, ever. I'm the one who opposed you. Your anger should be taken out on me."

Nyx studied David for a good solid minute. David started to wonder if the goddess was waiting for him to crumble under the pressure. Without a word, Nyx lifted her hand, and the pool at her feet began to overflow, seeping up onto the floor where Acacia and David stood. Acacia was forcefully pulled down, her four paws rooted to the floor as the water iced up around her legs, locking her in place. David gasped as he felt the painfully cold water envelope his legs up to mid-calf, icing over. The water did not stop there; it continued up his body, cocooning him, drenching him in the stark numbness of night. It permeated through his clothes, through his skin, into the trails of his veins, soaking up the warmth of his blood and chilling it, causing everything inside to ache and scream. He struggled to keep his head up, but the water was crawling up around his chest, around his neck. He could just make out Acacia's muffled words of anguish calling for him through the water clogging his ears ... and then it washed over his face ...

Nyx felt someone tugging on her gown.

It is very hard to surprise a god, particularly one with the gift of prophecy. Yet as Nyx looked down at the small boy at her side, she saw something in his face she had yet to ever see. There was no longer emptiness in the boy's eyes. He stared fixedly at her, pulling at her dress, and he shook his head.

Now where did you learn that? Nyx thought. *Certainly not from me ...* She looked back at David, who was slowly succumbing to her power. *Is this mortal boy truly so strange, that he has awoken this sense of compassion in you? I was sure that I had cast out such frail emotions from my being.*

She turned back to her precious incarnation. "You must watch and learn, little one. This is a taste of the power you will inherit from me. Watch and bar yourself from emotion, for tenderheartedness will make you weak. You must wield your power without mercy."

Once again, Nyx was taken aback as the incarnation

grabbed the wrist of her free hand, holding it with more strength than he appeared to have. There was definitely power behind it, a shadow of her own, but his face was now stone-solid with anger.

"Stop it," the incarnation ordered.

Nyx froze, for this was the first time in as long as she could remember that someone else was giving her a command—and she was startled. She smirked. *How can I refuse an order from myself?*

She lowered her hand, and the water receded back into the pool, freeing both the mortal boy and the sphinx. David wheezed for air, and shivered from the lingering chill. He dropped to his knees, and Acacia, also freed, rushed to him, wrapping a wing around him for warmth.

Silliness, to be moved by such pathetic things. Nyx took hold of a length of her dress, and wrapped it around her incarnation like a blanket. The incarnation grew tired, yawned, and nestled down into the tide of her gown, buried away in the soft essence that was comforting solely to him. Nyx thought: *You were not created as I had expected, and you disappoint me in many ways. But you have at least shown you can command respect, and you continue to surprise even me … that is worth something.*

Nyx moved across the surface of the pool, and hovered close to David and Acacia. The sphinx hissed in defiance, but Nyx paid her no mind. She caressed

David's cheek with bitterly cold fingertips. "All my oracle said was that I would claim you, but it did not say it would be today, nor tomorrow. You're still young … not quite ripe. I don't have much use for a boy who is full of foolishness, and whose bravery is encouraged by unchangeable prophecies and dumb luck. Perhaps once life has wizened you to hardship and suffering, maybe you can be of use to me. For now, what I need is the special cunning that I was going to harvest. Unfortunately, all my work on the sphinx is undone. What will I do now?"

David gulped, expecting that she meant to extract his cunning, but he could see a wicked gleam in Nyx's eye that spoke that she had other plans already. Abruptly, a fold of her gown whipped violently, and out of it rolled Nico, looking like he had just come fresh out of being trampled by horses.

The fox-man coughed as he sat up, dusting off his coat. He winced as he moved his bruised body. "It's about time! Those barbaric humans, haven't they heard that twenty against one is poor sportsmanship? And that big stupid lizard, wait until I get my hands on—" He looked up, to see David and Acacia on one side, and Madam Nyx on the other. He was confounded, although he tried to not appear so. "Nyx, your blessedness, I see you have brought my cousin and her savage plaything to be dealt with. I did what you told me, as I'm sure you know, but that scoundrel got in my way, and—"

"And you did not retrieve my Shade, as I asked of you," Nyx finished for him.

The Teumessian's eyes were horror-filled, and he scrambled backwards. "No, no, your holiness! I ... I was going to! But he had this mystical stone, and it has powers, and he used them against me! I assure you, I did everything I could to fulfill your request. I cannot help it if—"

"We agreed that if you helped me gain the sphinx's knowledge, then you would become the cleverest being in the world. But you did not prevent the boy from confining my Shade to the Singing Stone. It would take too much time to begin the process on the sphinx again, for her will is healed and strong, too strong to break. Your will, however ... it would take only a short time to unravel."

Nico scuttled behind David's legs. "Please, take him! He's cleverer than I. He outsmarts me all the time! He's the one that ruined all of our plans!"

"He is not the one who made promises to me, and broke them. If I cannot have the wit of the most intelligent creature in the world, then I will make do with the second-most."

A tendril from Nyx's dress shot out, grabbing Nico by the ankle. It slowly dragged him towards her, as the fox kicked and howled. "Please! I'll make it up to you! Just give me another ..." His voice was drowned out as he vanished into Nyx's essence, imprisoned somewhere inside her form.

"Bye, Cousin," Acacia said with a small wave of her paw.

David would have been happy for Nico's punishment, except he was concerned with what Nyx would do with them now.

Nyx sighed, stretching her wings. "I grow tired. It took much of my remaining energy to bring you here. I must preserve what strength I have left, and tend to my incarnation for now. I have more talents ready to collect, after all." She turned and began to ascend back up into the inky black universe.

"Are you letting us go?" David asked, even though he worried that might be a stupid thing to say.

Nyx turned back to him. "Did you want to stay for dinner?"

Taken aback by the question, not sure if it was a joke or not, David shyly shook his head.

Nyx returned to him, locking her gaze with his. She cupped his chin in her hand, turning his face from side to side. "You know, my incarnation will need beauty one of these days. You're a rather handsome boy."

David held his breath, petrified.

"Still … not quite ripe yet." She released him, and pressed a fingertip to his nose. "Pray that you grow ugly."

The next thing David and Acacia knew, they were falling down rapidly, and landed with a heavy sploosh into cold water. They paddled furiously back up to the surface, to find they were in the ocean, outside of Yofune's lair. They swam to the cave's edge, and climbed up onto warm, dry rock. Acacia shook herself like a drenched cat, spraying David with cold droplets. David plopped onto his back, feeling the sun warming his skin. Acacia curled up next to him in the comforting sunlight.

As they lay there, catching their breath, David said, "Well, this has been a busy day, hasn't it?"

CHAPTER EIGHTEEN

——— ✦ ———

Paris, a picturesque portrait of color and light, waited to welcome David under the morning sun, but anticipation and regret pulled him in opposing directions. He was standing in a field several miles from the infamous city, although the gateway from the Curtain that had returned him to this part of France had been about a day's journey behind him. He had been escorted by the caravan, including Yofune in human form and Tanuki, everyone wanting to spend what short time they had left with David to make it an enjoyable sending-off party. After Acacia had returned to the sirens' island and the special pocket in the Curtain to collect the wagons, the caravan was back to its full gloriously-colored train, with its white horses in the lead.

Each gypsy gave David a small gift to remember them by, in the forms of trinkets, woven clothing, and handmade talismans. Gullin did his best to keep an unreadable expression as he removed something from his belt. "There's something I'd like you to have. A little reminder of ol' Gullin." He held out a familiar silver rod.

268

"Orthrus? How did you get this back?" David asked. "I thought it was taken by the Lakota."

"Quick fingers," Gullin replied with a grin. "You didn't expect me to sit out in those woods all night with nothing to protect myself with?"

"You really want me to have it? No, I couldn't."

"Hey, I want this back someday," Gullin explained. "This is just to make sure I see you again so you can give it back." He winked, playfully mussing up David's hair. "Take care of yourself, boyo."

Yofune approached David, but Tanuki cut in front of him to grab the boy by the trouser leg. The badger sniffed back tears. "Do you have to leave already? Didn't you like my home? We could drink sake all day, go play tricks on the bandits some more, and we could go to the cherry blossom festival next month! Kyoto's festivals have the best bean-paste buns in all of Japan!"

David bent down to scratch Tanuki behind the ear. "It sounds wonderful, but I have an apprenticeship here, and I'm already late getting to it."

Tanuki furrowed his brows and frowned. "That old shaman said that I'm your spirit guide, and I say you can't go!"

"Tanuki," Yofune reprimanded him, and the badger reluctantly released David's leg. "David-san has been through much. It is time he goes back to his life. Wish him well."

Tanuki sniffled, folded his paws together and bowed. "I will miss you, David-san."

"As will I," Yofune agreed, also bowing. "You are a very special young man, David. You are blessed with much greatness and courage. You will carry those blessings with you throughout your journeys."

David picked up the badger gently, cradling him like a lapdog. "Don't be sad, everyone. We'll see each other again. After all, someone very special told me, 'don't make your goodbyes permanent.'"

It dawned on him that the hardest goodbye, the one for the person who had taught him that valuable piece of advice, was about to happen. David placed Tanuki down as he stepped forward, and the group parted. Standing in the back of the crowd, silent even though her voice was restored, Acacia watched David approach her. She forced a smile, but it could not mask her grief.

David reached for her right paw, holding it with no revulsion, no uncertainty. "Acacia, I'm very glad we met. I know you think that you shouldn't have brought me into your world, but you've taught me things I couldn't have ever begun to figure out on my own. And I won't forget them, I promise."

"You could, you know," she replied. "Forget all this. I haven't tried it yet, but if I can go into your dreams, I could probably rearrange a few memories. I could bury all this deeply enough that you won't remember, or make it all seem like just a dream, or have you think this was a last minute holiday with new friends. You don't have to forget Gullin, or my family or the others. You'd just forget me, and Nyx and Nico, and all that mess. I'll see to it that Nyx never comes after you ..." A deep, dark shadow crossed her face as she said this, "but you don't need to have the burden of her on your mind. It would be easier for you to forget."

David did not reply at first, for he was saddened that Acacia would consider wiping her image from his memory. "I think someone told me that even painful memories have something to teach us, for the better. Do you know what's even worse than a painful memory?" He locked his eyes with Acacia, memorizing the gorgeous golden swirls of her irises. "No memory at all."

The sphinx nodded. "How did you get so wise?"

David shrugged. "I have been spending a good deal of time with a sphinx lately. Perhaps something rubbed off on me. Who knows, I may wake up tomorrow with a coat of fur and a pair of wings."

The memory David would carry with him for the rest of his life, through his adulthood, through his old age, even when other fragments of his journey would eventually fade from his thoughts, was Acacia's laugh, clear and brazen and melodious, her happiness that had awaited centuries to finally be heard and be free.

David went on to his apprenticeship under Monsieur

Roland, learning the fine points of architecture until he proved to be quite the prodigy of design. He was given his own living quarters in a wing of the estate, and he often performed odd jobs for the Roland family to earn and save up extra money. It was not long until Monsieur Roland had him involved in many different aspects of his company, and David learned how to gain the trust of investors and how to make wise investments.

In his free time, David began to write stories, of sirens hosting festivals on hidden islands, and mischievous kappas who tricked evil-doers and loved cucumbers, and dragons from different parts of the world who battled one another, and of the magical white bison who helped people in need. When Mademoiselle Roland accidentally bumped David's desk one afternoon, spilling his latest manuscript onto the floor, she took a curious peek at the pages. Immediately she fell in love with his stories, and convinced David to send one of them to a close friend of hers, Louis Hachette, who owned the Hachette Livre publishing company. A letter arrived for David shortly thereafter, stating that Hachette Livre desired to publish his collection of stories. His book sold well—not fantastically, but well—and he became a prominent presence at many bookshops throughout Paris, signing books and giving talks to bibliophiles from every corner of the city.

David's greatest artistic accomplishment, though, was in the form of a meticulously drawn design that he showed Monsieur Roland when the elder architect was assisting another landscape architect to redesign the garden of the Tuileries Palace. The Tuileries Garden was a lush space adorned with statues reflecting famous Grecian themes, including one of Pegasus and another of Theseus and the Minotaur. Roland smiled at David's proposal, commended him for the ingenuity, but he filed the drawing among his papers and it was to remain dormant for many a year.

Miraculously, several decades later, the proposal would resurface as to what statues should be placed by the quay in the Tuileries Gardens, and just as ancient Thebes had once had one of flesh at its gates, so sphinxes of stone were constructed to welcome visitors to the gardens. It was not the same design as David's; these sphinxes were based more on the Egyptian model, with a pharaoh's headdress and no wings, but they have remained steadfast sentinels in the garden to this day.

There was one thing that bothered David, from time to time. He dreamed often of the beautiful woman with the long dark hair, and the green eyes rimmed in gold, waiting for him on the grassy shore overlooking the sea. Yet, in none of these dreams could he ever quite reach her, quite hear her, as she always was just outside of his range, an invisible field between them. What frustrated him was that he could not tell: was she truly there, trying to speak to him in his dreams and having trouble doing so, or were these only manifestations of his own imagination, his own hopes and desires? If it was the latter, was she not coming to see him in his sleep at all? Had she forgotten about him?

Gradually, the dreams became less and less frequent, until his dreams were consumed with daily matters, or inspirations for new stories he could write. Eventually, the images of sphinxes masquerading as human vanished altogether.

David made constant trips on behalf of Monsieur Roland, for acquiring new clients and maintaining good relations with longtime investors. One such trip took him to Barcelona, where after finishing business matters, he paid a long-anticipated visit to the nearby Fernandez estate, where he was warmly welcomed by a very enthusiastic Catarina Fernandez Flores.

"We were so happy to receive your message that you were visiting!" she exclaimed as she embraced David in a tight hug. "It's been so long since we've heard from you. I feared I was never going to see you again."

"I'm afraid I've gotten lackadaisical in my viola practice," David said, "but I was hoping you could refresh my memory a bit."

Catarina smiled, noting the brand new black case in the shape of her beloved instrument tucked protectively under his arm. For nearly three years out of practice, he was not bad.

Into the second year of his apprenticeship, David was on a business trip in London to meet with a new prospective client who wished to commission the Roland Company to design a grand layout for a public park. He had arrived in the late afternoon, and feeling parched, took a brisk walk down a main street to find a watering hole.

There were plenty of restaurants and taverns in this area, but his eye caught one called The Hunter's Dogs. What was particular about the pub's sign was its depiction of the titular dogs, for it was a full bodied profile of one wolfhound, with a second one masked behind it except for its head. It looked like a two-headed dog.

David thought of the silver tube with the wolves' heads on each end, tucked away in a safe at his home.

He entered the pub. It was a rollicking place, as a group of mill workers were gathered around singing old tunes in a corner while downing pints of ale. David sat down at a table, ordered a drink, and waited patiently for something, he was not sure what.

It was not long before someone clasped him roughly on the shoulder.

"Looks like the pup's become a stud, eh, boyo?" laughed the rough voice with the Scottish brogue.

Gullin yanked David up out of his chair in a hearty

hug, slapping him on the back. The Scotsman was as lively and rugged as ever, and not much different except for a slightly more protruding belly. He sat down at David's table and ordered a round of ale for them both, his treat.

They spent the next hour discussing their lives from the past two years. David briskly explained his professional successes, and Gullin imparted his tales of various jobs and journeys, most of them unusually "normal" given his background. While he was still technically a member of the Master Huntsmen society, he had fallen out of league with them and rarely saw anything of the supernatural variety anymore. Most of his hunting, nowadays, was purely to sell in the marketplace, pheasants and deer and boar. That was more hobby than vocation, as he was no longer a wandering man.

"Got myself a lass now," Gullin said proudly. "Beatrice is a true fire-spark. She can tackle a bear about as well as I, and she's thrice as ferocious when she wants to be. We've got a wee one on the way."

"That's wonderful, Gullin. It's hard to picture you a family man, I admit."

Gullin smirked. "Was a bit odd to settle down, at first. But it feels nice, having someone there in your arms when you fall asleep, and to kiss you when you wake up. I had almost forgot what that felt like."

"Is that why you left the caravan?" David asked. "You wanted a quiet life, with a family of your own?"

Gullin gulped down what was left in his third round of ale before answering. "Truth is, everyone in the caravan parted ways. Some folks joined up with larger caravans, some took their chances to go west to America. Two or three of the young lasses found themselves some well-to-do lads and became happy brides."

David was surprised to hear this. "Why did you all leave? You were family to each other."

"And we always will be, don't be fooled. Just that … well," Gullin scratched his head, with a puzzled look on his face. "Things change, boyo. The mistress … Acacia … felt like she was keeping us from living normal lives. She said she wanted us to have the things everyone has, and that she felt like she was dragging us around without any purpose. She made sure we were all taken care of, gave us all our fair shares and earnings. I think she even set up Isabella with a good rich suitor, by going into this fellow's dreams and making him think of Isabella all the time until he proposed. She cut herself out of most of the folks' memories, so they don't remember the Curtain or nothing, except for me. I refused it. Don't think she would've been able to make me forget everything anyway."

Sadness pierced David's heart. "Acacia's all alone? Where did she go?"

Gullin shrugged. "No sayin'. She doesn't dream-talk with me no more, so I can't say where she's been. But I think there was more to it, than just wanting us to have normal lives. I think she was planning something for some time, something she had to do by herself and didn't want us to get caught up in. An enigma, as always. Best of luck to her." He raised his empty glass in toast, and David clinked his glass in agreement.

"I don't suppose you are going to ask for me to return Orthrus?" David asked with a grin. "You said that the next time I saw you, you'd want it back."

Gullin waved his hand at David. "Keep it. I don't have any need for something like that. I ain't been caught inside no dragons' mouths lately," he laughed, clapping David on the shoulder. His hand lingered there for a moment, and he gave David's shoulder a light squeeze. "It was good to see you again, boyo."

David raised an eyebrow at him. "Let's be honest with each other, Gullin. You never really liked me."

Gullin sighed. "In the guild, I was trained to be the best of the best. We were the monster slayers, the tamers of the most powerful beasts. It was hard to see someone who could do what I couldn't do, who could save the one thing on earth I wanted to save. Envy can make a man a fool sometimes. But we were part of the same pack. That made us brothers." He stood up from his chair. "*Makes* us brothers. But I'll still whoop you if I think you need it, don't forget it."

"Hey, I fought a Teumessian fox, if you remember. Don't think I can't hold my own," David reminded him.

"Eh, and neither of us could hold our own against

Beatrice," Gullin laughed, slapping David on the back again. "By the by, I expect next time I see you that you have yourself a good lass. Build yourself a hat shop to lure 'em in, if you have to."

David nodded, but he couldn't say that deep down, there was still a small piece of his heart that he couldn't give away to another woman, not yet. He had come to accept that Catarina was married and well, and he was happy for her. But how can you let go of the last fragment of magic, the final piece of wonderment from a woman who was bound to your dreams? How could you give up the feelings of the one person in the world, in two worlds, who you were destined to save? Didn't that, by purest definition, mean you were tied to that person for your whole life?

But Acacia had released the others, allowed them the freedom to live as people should. She had released him too, so to save him from the wrath of Nyx—although it was yet to be determined if the goddess was planning to return for him. Perhaps, he needed to put those days of peril and mystery behind him. There may be something else, something he could not foresee or plan, awaiting him.

When he returned to Paris, something was indeed waiting for him. One day shortly thereafter, a pretty young strawberry-blonde Englishwoman approached him in a bookstore. She sparked a conversation about the impact of folklore on ancient cultures, but he was paying more attention to her lovely green eyes that matched her parsley-colored petticoat.

She asked, with a bubbly giddiness, "I've read your stories, Mr. Sandoval, and I love to read them aloud to my book group. They seem so lifelike, as if you had actually been to those exotic places. In fact ..." She dropped her gaze in coy embarrassment. "One of the reasons I moved here from Bristol was hoping I might meet you someday."

A few months later, David proposed to the young lady, Florence, and she happily accepted. Between David's saved income and Florence's dowry, they were able to buy a lovely flat nearby the Paris Opera. Many evenings the soul-stirring music from the opera house flew on the evening breeze and found its way into their home, promising that their new life together would always be beautiful.

Not long after David's engagement, he received an odd package on his doorstep.

It was a long but thin package, and it was obvious it had not come with the evening post. He carried the wrapped bundle inside to the parlor, sat down on the settee, untied the twine and stripped away the brown paper. Beneath was a smooth polished wooden box, and inside of it was an intricately designed sheath of ebony detailed with silver, and inside this sheath was a finely crafted sword that curved like a basilisk's tongue. It was a perfect matching partner to the dagger he had left behind in America with the Lakota when he had searched for Ptesan-Wi—until he looked back down in the box, and there it was, that very dagger.

With these gifts was a note tied up with a white ribbon. Unfurling it, David read:

Dear David,

I came across an old friend of yours in the Americas, who has been holding onto your lost dagger. She said that she was able to get it back from the Lakota, and when she passed it along to me, I thought you might like a new partner to go along with it. Something old, something new. I'll leave it to your beautiful bride-to-be to find something borrowed and something blue.

Don't think that I have forgotten you. I write to you now because of the path you have set me on, and I want to thank you for giving me a purpose yet again. You gave me a second chance, but there are many out there, from the hidden side of the Curtain, who are still plagued by Nyx's Shades and will lose their essences and lives to her. Since I was spared, it is only right that I do all I can to stop her and save my brethren from an undeserved fate. That is why I am gathering those that wish to join me, to seek out those who are plagued and to find other talismans on earth that can seal the Shades of Nyx away forever. As you must know by now, I gave all of my family their freedom, to be safe and happy, to not be endangered by the mission I now undertake.

I will not allow Nyx to come back for you, and she knows this. Yet she still wields influences on others with weak wills and tainted hearts. The second reason I am writing this is to make you aware of why I have sent you your dagger and this sword. You may find yourself needing to use them someday ...

Know that I will never be far from you. Know that while, for your safety, I cannot communicate with you in your dreams because of Nyx, you will remain in my thoughts. And know that I am happy for you, for your new love and your beautiful life. You will always have a part of me with you, and I love you.

--Acacia

David folded the note as tenderly as if it were a wounded bird, and placed it back in the box with the sword and dagger. He sat in silence for a long time, looking out the window at a box garden displayed on the ledge. He smiled at the occupant of the flower box, a plant that had been difficult for him to have shipped from far away. It was bound not to last long since it was foreign, and the soil and temperature were not quite right. Yet somehow, defying adversity, it had blossomed well, as its tiny golden petals bloomed among its thorny stems.

He gazed a while longer at his acacia plant. He stood up with his precious gift and walked out towards the dining room, where he knew Florence was reading the first draft of his latest children's book about the funny tender-hearted badger who could turn into a rain-cloud, since she loved those stories the best.

EPILOGUE

Free. Finally free.

The dark, the wet, and the cold had been his cellmates for the length of a hundred lifetimes. All three clung to his steel-gray fur, stiffening his flesh and bones, commanding that he stay in his subterranean cell. But the ribbon was finally broken, after centuries of its supposedly unyielding resilience. If he could not distance himself from this prison quickly, his captors would be upon him with the force of lightning and earthquake. If they discovered that he could no longer be contained, they would destroy him.

His legs fired like pistons. His lungs ached from all the years of pumping icy air and stale dust, and they burned as fresh, warm air greeted them in his flight. So many parts of him burned: his eyes from the light, his nose from the million new scents, and his blood for raging, ravenous revenge.

His nose sniffed the winds. *The world smells so different.*

His ears twitched at the cacophony that echoed from all corners of the land. *The world sounds so different.*

The world. I despise it.

He had always hated the world. Not that the world itself had ever done anything to him, other than force him to live in it. He had been born with the sole purpose to devour it one day. He couldn't possibly love the world if his existence demanded that he would end it.

Not yet, though. There were things to be done first. He would devour that fool Lawkeeper who tied the ribbon on him, dooming him to an eternity of solitude. He would devour the fool gods who thought he could be locked away. Then, with great relish, he would devour the world, the moon, the sun, and anything else he craved.

His tongue slid into the empty notch of his teeth that had once displayed his most prized feature. *My fang. How I have waited to reclaim you.*

He had heard whispers trickle down through the cracks of the earth while he had been decaying in his prison. He had heard rumors about what had been done with his fang. Had he known that his fang would have snagged in the Lawkeeper's wrist and been torn clean from his mouth, he never would have bitten off the traitor's hand to begin with.

The whispers had spoken of his fang being transformed, smithed into a wondrous dagger. The whispers had rumored that because it was his fang, it might be the only weapon in the world that could kill him.

He had to find his fang. He needed it if he was to consume those who had betrayed him. He had to ensure there was nothing, and no one, out there who could pose a threat to his quest.

The whispers had once mentioned, very softly, very provocatively, that his fang may have fallen into the possession of the last living sphinx …

NICK HAWTHORNE AND THE BANEFIRES OF AUTUMN

Book 1
The Albion Chronicles

by

Craig Booker

PROLOGUE

Deep in the bowels of the Earth, following a tortuous, winding journey through the dark, narrow defiles of Albion's Northern Shire, Sir Benedict Harkness, hereditary peer of that land, bartered with mad Crystaljack over the legendary Crystal Rings.

"Four I have," muttered the deranged hermit, shifting uneasily in his grimy grey rags, "and four I'll keep. They're mine. I won't relinquish any of 'em, to you or anybody else who happens to come calling. Not a single one, you hear?"

"You must! The future of Albion is at stake!" The flickering candlelight rippled back and forth across the aristocrat's lean, handsome features, and the rich tones of his voice echoed through the hermit's den. The two were seated opposite one another, amongst the musty tomes and cobweb-bedecked paraphernalia Crystaljack purported to use. All was quiet, save for their hushed voices, and the splutter and crackle of the oily brands set into the walls.

"You know that they must be given freely," Crystaljack sneered. "They can't be taken by force."

"I am aware of that." Sir Benedict leaned forward suddenly and grasped the hermit's only arm by its filthy wrist. He held it near to the candle flame, and the four rings, one on each grimy, stunted finger, sparkled like freshly cut gems, although their stones were of an altogether different nature.

"Let me go!" squeaked Crystaljack; but Sir Benedict did not. Instead, gripping the other's scrawny wrist even more tightly, the aristocrat responded.

"Are you deaf, hermit? Do you not understand the import of what I say? Listen, aye, and listen closely. The darkness is gathering. The time of the Evil One is nigh. Our fair land of Albion is entering the darkest, most perilous phase of her existence. We are in danger; such peril that the world itself may not recover from such a catastrophe. But if we act now, we may still have time to avert it. I need your help, Crystaljack. I need one of your rings, and I need to take it and go now!"

"*My* help?" The hermit wheezed, his eyes narrowing. "No-one needs Crystaljack's help. I think you're lying, Sir Aristocrat, Sir Lord of the Manor."

"It is Beacon Night in six weeks. If we cannot prevent the rise of the Evil One by then, we are all lost. You are as doomed as the rest of us, make no mistake. Not even the Rings will save you if we fail to wake the Lady."

"If I can't save myself with my Rings, then I fail to see how you can fare any better," argued Crystaljack reasonably.

"Our last hope lies in locating the Charm. This is why I need to borrow the Ring of Past Visions." Sir Benedict ground his teeth in an effort to keep his voice steady.

"The Charm. Stuff of legend, that."

"All my efforts to locate the Charm have proven fruitless, yet still my brother, the Eyes of the Wind, ranges the shires of England in search of It. And without the Charm, we are surely doomed. But with the aid of the Ring of Past Visions…"

Crystaljack shook his arm free and grunted. "What? And the Ring will give you a chance? A chance to save this precious Albion of yours? You're even more insane than I am! Anyway, what do I care for Albion? She cares little enough for me."

"She cares for all, hermit. Now, you know your duty. Give me the Ring."

"Crystaljack didn't ask to be brought into this world, this Albion," replied the hermit, staring lopsidedly at his visitor. "Therefore, what does he owe in return? Nothing. What's more, I don't even have the same advantages as most others. A single arm and half a brain." He snorted, and then giggled as if he found this fact perversely amusing.

"You know that I speak the truth." Sir Benedict's

eyes transfixed Crystaljack's coal black orbs; his words, spoken softly now, had a far greater impact than if he had yelled.

"No I don't," snapped the other; but he looked away sharply.

Sir Benedict smiled. "Well, Mad Crystaljack; you have the means at your disposal to prove otherwise."

The shabby figure picked its nose, affecting disdain and disinterest. "What if I have?"

"Then use it."

"Ugh. A trick." The hermit squinted hideously.

"The Ring of Absolute Integrity can be used to verify the truthfulness of any statement, as well you know." Sir Benedict glanced down casually at a bright yellow stone which winked and sparkled in the uncertainty of the candleglow.

The other looked wistful for a moment. "Aye; that it can. And it has been a while since I used it. Very well, Sir Aristocrat." Slowly he brought his hand forward. "Touch the stone. Quickly, now; before I change my mind!"

Sir Benedict complied. Immediately his long fingers touched the cool, smooth surface, he felt a stirring, as if he had awakened something best left undisturbed. Then it seemed as if the room had tilted, and his head began to tingle and swim; but still he held the other's gaze, and he did not break the contact, even though his senses threatened to leave him.

But then the stone burned to green, and the hermit

snatched his hand away, muttering and cursing to himself. "So you speak truthfully," he said at last, watching the gem fade quickly to yellow.

"The Ring shall be returned to you. This I promise on my family, and on my ancestors." He held his hand out for a second time, this time palm upward. "Give me the ring."

Crystaljack sniggered. "Oh, well," he said pettishly. "Take it. Take it, and I still have three. Truth to tell, there is only the Ring of Future Possibilities I wouldn't part with. That one brings madness. Too much to take in. Too much." With a dexterous movement he bent forward and clenched his teeth over the ring, which he drew from his finger and spat out on the table. Sir Benedict picked it up and wiped it hastily on his sleeve. Squinting narrowly, he held it close to the flickering flame to inspect it.

"I trust you have the skill to use it," said Crystaljack in a fawning, sarcastic tone.

"Oh, I have skills aplenty. This, I think, is not beyond me." He slipped the Magickal artefact smoothly over his third finger, marvelling at the fit. "I shall take my leave now, Crystaljack. The Ring of Past Visions will be returned to you after this Beacon Night." He pushed his chair away from the table and stood up, brushing the creases from his cloak. "Until next we meet, Sir Hermit."

Crystaljack watched the tall, handsome man as he strode purposefully away and began to ascend the stone stairwell to the surface. When his visitor had disappeared, he burst into a fit of giggles. "Three left, three left. I wonder which of them I shall use next?" His thumb brushed the blue one briefly, but then he shook his head. It was seldom a good idea to invoke the Ring of Chance Encounters.